Castrose Zukan returns to the hideaway his brother, Clayton, had been using, only to find it destroyed. After checking the escape route they'd created, he discovers Clayton didn't leave alone. While it takes a few days, Castrose figures out who took him . . . and where. He sneaks into the United States and heads to a little mountain town called Stone Ridge. What he doesn't expect is to become the hunted.

When Eion MacDougal watched his two eldest brothers and dozens of others in their wolf shifter pack find their mates, he never lost hope that he would find his own someday. Out hunting with family in wolf form, that day comes when he runs across a guy with a sniper rifle. Revealing himself has unexpected consequences. The big, blond human faints.

With help from his family, Eion takes him home. Help from his pack tells him who the human is . . . and why he's there. When Castrose wakes, can he win the man's trust? Or will his mate flee from Eion when he learns he's part of the group that kidnapped the human's only family?

In the Sniper's Crosshairs
Copyright © 2019 Charlie Richards
ISBN: 978-1-4874-2679-8
Cover art by Angela Waters

Published by eXtasy Books Inc or
Devine Destinies, an imprint of eXtasy Books Inc

Look for us online at:
www.eXtasybooks.com or www.devinedestinies.com

IN THE SNIPER'S CROSSHAIRS
WOLVES OF STONE RIDGE: BOOK FORTY-NINE

BY

CHARLIE RICHARDS

DEDICATION

So Matilda's strong young mind continued to grow, nurtured by the voices of all those authors who had sent their books out into the world like ships onto the sea. These books gave Matilda a hopeful and comforting message — you are not alone.
~from the movie Matilda

CHAPTER ONE

As soon as the buckle seatbelt light flashed off, Castrose Zukan unclipped the clasp and rose to his feet. He longed to stretch his arms over his head and pop his back, but he knew that would have to wait. Even flying first class, Castrose found the seats on the airplane uncomfortable for his big six-foot-three-inch frame.

Time to get off this damn bird, so I can stretch my legs.

Castrose grabbed his carry-on bag from the overhead storage bin. Slinging the satchel over his shoulder, he straightened his suit coat, then began making his way down the aisle toward the door. Even as big as he was, Castrose easily maneuvered around the other fliers and made it to the door nearly first.

Sometimes, military training came in handy in unexpected ways.

Slipping from the plane, Castrose strode steadily down the attached tunnel. He followed the tide of people toward the customs check and found a slow-moving line to stand in. When he finally reached the head of the line, Castrose pulled his fake identification from the inside pocket of his suit coat.

Castrose spotted a passenger moving away from a booth, so he headed that way. Offering a slight smile, he handed his identification to the attendant.

The man behind the counter read over the information, glanced at him, then placed a stamp on his passport. "Welcome to Houston, Mr. Randin. I hope you enjoy your stay."

"Thank you," Castrose replied, giving the man another

small smile as he took his passport back.

As Castrose moved away from the counter, he tucked his forged information back into his suit coat. His documents listed his name as Daniel Randin, a Swedish native who had diplomatic immunity. That meant his bag wouldn't be searched, allowing him to break down his sniper rifle and carry it on the plane with him.

While there was always the low chance of getting hassled, Castrose had chosen to take the chance. He'd been through so many custom checks that he'd learned what set off people's radar and knew to avoid that. In this instance, acting as a weary business traveler was a damn sure bet that he would be waved on through.

And I was right.

Without a bag to pick up and only having the clothes on his back and one change in his bag — which were wrapped around the pieces of his weapon — Castrose headed toward the car rental area. Once there, he had to stand in another line. Rubbing the back of his neck, he silently urged the rental company to open a second line.

Castrose almost chuckled when two minutes later, another employee appeared from the back and did just that. Within ten minutes, he'd used his forged documents to rent a four-wheel-drive pick-up truck. Evidently, in Texas, that was fairly common, so he even had his choice of blue, red, or black.

With keys in hand, Castrose left the airport. He found his vehicle in the slot the woman had indicated on the map. After placing his satchel on the floor of the passenger side, he climbed behind the wheel and fired it up.

As Castrose drove, he searched for a fast food joint. He hated plane food. First, it was never enough. Second, even in first class, it tasted like shit.

Spotting a sub sandwich place, Castrose hummed. "Oh, yeah. That's what I'm talkin' about," he mumbled. With a sigh of relief, he parked in the lot and hustled in to get a few sub sandwiches for the trip.

While Castrose could have caught a connecting flight and flown directly to Denver, he'd chosen to drive. He hated flying and crossing the ocean was long enough. Besides, it gave him time to wait for his contact in the CIA to get him the last of the information he needed.

There was something odd about how someone from a hick town had managed to infiltrate his brother's home.

Castrose still remembered the shock he'd felt when he'd driven to his hidden parking spot, hiked toward the abandoned cabin, and found the destruction of the home. His heart had skipped a beat, and he'd gasped. He'd swept his gaze over the devastation as he'd rubbed his chest.

His brother, his only family, had been in that cabin — Clayton Zukan.

While Castrose had learned bomb-making while in the military, his younger, much-smaller brother, had taken his training manuals and turned it into an art form. His bombs ended up in high demand. Turning his skills toward sniper-dom, Castrose had ended up a hell of a shot, and after leaving the military, combined with the martial arts training he'd enjoyed since he was five, he'd had an easy segue into becoming an assassin.

Castrose and Clayton had banded together and created a kickass team. It was a good thing his brother had a moral compass. Clayton laid the ground rules for who they sold to, who they allowed to hire them, and always demanded Castrose confirm that what the client said had happened was actually the truth.

Without Clayton, Castrose knew he would lose those values. He had never considered himself a bad man, but he certainly wouldn't be called good, either.

I need my brother.

Fortunately, Castrose had located the exit of their underground lair's escape tunnel. While the opening itself was charred from the flames of the explosion, the land itself had given him plenty of clues. He had found tracks . . . a lot of tracks. Castrose recognized his brother had left one of the sets.

Thanks to the maker.

Collecting his discreetly placed cameras, Castrose had felt a wealth of relief to discover that not only was Clayton alive, but he was also uninjured. Hell, the group who'd escorted him to a hidden SUV hadn't even trussed him. In fact, Clayton had been chatting eagerly with them, appearing to question them and get responses in return.

Just who the fuck are these guys? And why didn't Clayton leave me a message?

Castrose had holed up in a hotel room and spent several days watching the sites where his brother might reach out to him. In the meantime, he had delved into their recent accepted assignments. If someone had managed to track Castrose and Clayton to their secret hideaway in Romania, then they had to be very good, have a lot of money, or perhaps both.

In conjunction with that, Castrose had cross-referenced everyone in the person or person's life with acquaintances, friends, or family.

It had taken Castrose three days to spot a correlation.

Clayton had accepted a bomb contract from the Danner family. According to his brother's research, the sibling pair was going to get revenge on an assassin who'd taken their money, then warned their father — who they'd hired him to kill because the man had threatened to cut them out of his will since they were no-good lay-abouts. While the premise was admirable — sort of — backstabbing in the assassin industry just wasn't done.

Castrose understood why the siblings — who had ended up in prison — had wanted retribution. Since Clayton had taken the contract, he figured his brother had agreed. What Castrose couldn't figure out was how the assassin's husband's co-workers had tracked down Clayton.

Guess I'll figure that out when I get there.

To that end, Castrose had asked an associate for information on the residents of Stone Ridge. He'd been shocked when the other man had come back with very little. The group was all very insular, taking care of their own and dealing with problems in their own way.

It sort of reminded him of the local authorities in the first *John Rambo* movie. The backwoods sheriff had a bone to pick with a stranger, and he'd utilized all his resources to take him down. While it hadn't worked so well for the hick in that movie—and in this case, Castrose would substitute a forest ranger for the sheriff—the premise was still dangerously similar.

One of the ranger's officers—Carson Angeni—had died due to someone going after his husband. The husband had been Jared Templeton, the assassin who'd taken the money. He'd dropped off the grid and gotten out of the business over ten years before, but someone had still wanted him eliminated, and he and Clayton had taken the job.

Evidently, everyone at that office was close. Hell, only the year before they'd lost another ranger to a forest fire that had taken out the man's home, killing his wife and daughter along with him—Shane and his family. The head ranger, Declan McIntire, obviously didn't take kindly to losing another of his men.

Another big difference seemed to be how connected Declan was for a forest ranger. He must have had some serious skill— or one of his people did—to get information on Castrose. He wasn't even certain who would have been skilled enough to locate Clayton's hideout.

On top of all that, how the bomb had ended up in Jared and Carson's home as opposed to their rental car when they'd taken a trip to Los Angeles, Castrose had no clue.

Just something else to figure out.

Shaking his head as Castrose climbed back into his rented truck, he settled comfortably behind the wheel. After placing the bag containing the six sub sandwiches on his lap, he peered into the paper sack. Castrose rifled through the offerings he'd ordered — two roast beef, two turkeys, one ham, and one pastrami — and chose one of the turkey subs.

All the sandwiches were lightly baked, so the cheese was melted and the bread toasted. He'd asked for extra veggies, including lettuce, tomatoes, cucumbers, and green peppers, as well as extra mayo. He'd even gone ahead and had them add a few jalapeno slices to the sandwiches.

As Castrose unwrapped the top half of the sandwich, using the wrapper as a holder, his stomach rumbled in anticipation. He licked his lips, then took a huge bite. Chewing slowly, he groaned appreciatively as he enjoyed the myriad of flavors bursting over his tongue.

Exquisite. Love toasted flatbread.

With his food in his left hand, Castrose used his right to spread a napkin over his lap. Then he awkwardly opened a bag of harvest cheddar *Sun Chips* and tucked it between his thighs. Once he had his food settled, he fired up the truck and, once again, started on his way.

After five hours, a second sandwich, and one stop to piss and get fuel, Castrose pulled into a chain hotel. He paid for a room, then locked himself into it. After a shower and getting cleaned up, he dropped into bed and passed out.

Castrose was on the road again, bright and early. After another half a day of travel, he spotted the road sign for Stone Ridge — thirty-seven miles. Turning left, he began his ascent deeper into the mountains.

As Castrose peered left and right, he took in the dense growth of trees. His mind strayed to the email he'd received from his associate that morning. He couldn't hide his shock that the man had told him that he could no longer continue researching Declan and his people.

Orders from his boss. What the hell?

Killian Obskund worked in intelligence for the United States. Why the hell would someone in the CIA tell Killian to stop looking into a backwoods park ranger?

Castrose didn't know, but the strange turn of events caused the hairs on his nape to stand on end. He couldn't remember the last time he'd felt a spike of nerves so great. If it hadn't been his brother in trouble, Castrose would have walked away.

Except, he couldn't.

He's my only family.

Heaving a sigh, Castrose spotted the sign *Welcome to Stone Ridge – Population four hundred seventy-two.* He figured most people had to live amidst the winding mountain roads because the town itself was tiny. Castrose had heard the expression, *if you blink, you'll miss it,* and he could see that it completely applied.

There was a large local market, a police station, a fire station, and according to the sign, the post office was on a side street. There was the requisite pizza parlor, frosty and burger joint, and a family diner. The town even had a bar and grill – Caribou's – which boasted the best hot wings and cheese fries on the mountain.

Castrose's stomach growled at the idea of greasy goodness.

Instead of giving in to his belly's need, Castrose stopped at a gas station. He fueled his pick-up and grabbed a pre-made sub sandwich, a canister of French onion *Pringles*, and a six-pack of bottled water. As he paid for everything, he realized he was going to have to do a hell of a lot of sit-ups to burn off all the carbs he'd eaten over the last few days.

The upcoming hike into the forest should help.

For the next two hours, Castrose drove around the mountain roads. He found Declan's driveway, as well as the homes of his other park rangers—Nick Greely and Dixon Holsteen. Castrose even found the remains of Carson Angeni and Jared Templeton's home.

Castrose frowned as he stared at the destruction. There was something about it . . . something that niggled at his senses. Unwilling to stay too long and be noticed, Castrose filed his discontent away to peruse another time.

He would figure out what was bothering him . . . eventually.

"Okay, time to explore the logging roads," Castrose muttered as he circled back around and once again located Declan's home. "Let's see if I can't find a good location to scope out your place."

With that thought in mind, Castrose turned left onto the first available dirt road. He didn't get far. There was a gate with a chain and lock, so he found a spot to turn around, returned to the street, and tried again.

Although Castrose could have hiked in, he felt his truck would have been left too close to the road. He had better luck on the next road. While there were plenty of grasses and weeds springing up the middle of the dirt and gravel track, it extended a good half mile into the woods before petering out.

In fact, at the end, Castrose spotted a small parking area and a sign indicating it was the head of a hiking trail.

"Perfect." Castrose smiled grimly. He remembered that Declan McIntire's fifty-plus acre plot backed up to BLM property and National Forest lands. If the satellite mapping app on his phone worked way out there, Castrose bet he could easily scout it out.

After packing his food and water into his duffel bag, Castrose placed the strap over his shoulder. He locked up his pick-up, shoved the keys into his pocket, and headed to the trailhead sign. As he read the map indicating the trail—a six-mile strenuous hike with plenty of elevation change, which explained why the place was so overgrown—Castrose tried to pull up his map.

Castrose grinned.

It works.

Between the board's map and his phone, Castrose plotted out a route.

Of course, the second he started the trail, he realized his folly. Hiking through unfamiliar woods was completely different than picking a straight direction on a map.

Oh, well. Good thing I have plenty of food and water. I'm gonna be at this awhile.

CHAPTER TWO

Snorting upon hearing his youngest brother's joke, Eion MacDougal nudged his elbow into him. He rolled his eyes as he quipped back, "Yeah, you and what army?" Waggling his brows, Eion added, "I'll let you decide on our pairs. Whoever you want to match us with, me and whoever will still take down a bigger game animal than you all."

After finishing that parting shot, Eion crossed his arms over his chest and lifted one brow. He gave Brennan an imperious look. His youngest brother was a damn fine hunter in his own right, but he and his wolf had never had any trouble tracking and taking down some game — whether he had help or not.

Eion was the best tracker in his family behind his eldest brother. Cliff was their wolf shifter pack's head tracker, having taken over from their father, Duncan. Their father had been the head tracker for over two centuries. It was a family position that they'd been able to earn first in Ireland. Then, after Alpha Declan McIntire had taken over the pack from his grandfather, Duncan had spent years learning their new territory in Stone Ridge, Colorado, before sharing his knowledge with each of his children.

"Then you hunt with Niamh, and I'll hunt with Cliff." Brennan crossed his arms over his chest, smirking at him as if daring him to counter his declaration.

Humming, Eion bit back his chuckle. He nodded slowly. Even after over a hundred years of being siblings, he realized Brennan still hadn't learned.

While Cliff was their pack's lead tracker, Brennan should have taken into account the fact that their brother's mate was pregnant—very pregnant—with their second child. There was no way that Cliff would be able to focus on a hunt. On top of that, for some reason that Eion had never fathomed, Brennan always believed their sisters weren't as good at hunting.

Nothing could have been further from the truth.

Both Niamh and Brielle—his older and younger sisters respectively—were fantastic hunters. Just because both female shifters had found their mates at an early age and settled down to raise cubs, that didn't make them weak. Instead, in Eion's opinion, that made his sisters even tougher.

As wolf shifters, they would be even better at hunting game, since they would have a driving need not only to feed their pups but also to keep them safe.

"When are we doing this?" Eion asked, keeping his tone level as he brought his glass of iced tea to his lips. He took a swallow, waiting for his impetuous brother's answer.

Grinning, Brennan replied, "This afternoon."

Eion couldn't help but betray his surprise, lifting his left brow. He knew his brother would know from his scent, too.

Okay.

"Stakes?" Eion just knew his brother had to want something big for him to push in such a way.

Brennan's confidence slipped a bit, and he lowered his arms. He shifted his weight from foot to foot. After a glance to the left, Brennan seemed to catch himself.

Jutting his chin into the air, Brennan crossed his arms over his chest again. "I get your *Harley* for an evening."

Eion's initial response was to refuse. No way in hell did he want to allow Brennan to use his motorcycle . . . for any length of time. The vintage *Harley Panhead* had been his baby for decades . . . not to mention that Brennan's driving sucked—in a car, truck, or otherwise.

Biting off his initial response, Eion growled, "What the hell do you want with my *Panhead*?"

Clearing his throat, Brennan rubbed the back of his neck. Once again, his discomfort came through loud and clear. Then his cheeks took on a pinkish hue.

"Good grief," Eion muttered, his mind quickly making an educated guess. "Does this have something to do with you trying to get laid?"

Brennan opened his mouth, then immediately closed it again. His cheeks darkened further, making his green eyes appear to glow. He cleared his throat but didn't say anything.

Eion heaved a deep sigh. "Gods. Seriously? You know my *Panhead* doesn't seat two."

Well, not comfortably, anyway.

There was no bitch seat on the bike, although a couple of times over the years, Eion had put a date on his lap. That had been decades ago, however. Back before the government had implemented all kinds of safety laws.

Not that he wouldn't do it anyway if he wanted to. The law enforcement around Stone Ridge was mostly fellow shifters. He knew they wouldn't give him shit about it.

Of course, Eion didn't currently have a special someone to feel tempted to break the law with.

As a wolf shifter, a creature who shared his spirit with a wolf and could change into the animal at will, Eion was considered a paranormal. His kind lived upward of five hundred years. To relieve the possible monotony and loneliness, Fate created a soul mate for them . . . someone they could bond with and share their life thread with.

Finding him or her, however, was the trick.

Over the last decade or so, Eion had watched many of the shifters around Stone Ridge find their fated mate. He hadn't been that fortunate, yet. Eion hoped that would change someday soon.

"I'm not gonna take her on the bike," Brennan claimed. "I

just wanna impress her." His eyes narrowed as he peered over Eion's shoulder. "She thinks they're cool."

Eion inhaled slowly, then let the breath out just as slowly. "Gods, you're lying to me," he grumbled, crossing his arms over his chest. "Your scent is totally giving you away." Shaking his head, Eion scowled at his brother. "You've been spending too much time with humans." He knew Brennan spent a lot of his spare time with his co-workers as opposed to family. "You lie to your buddies like that, too?"

He was more than happy to call out his baby brother.

Huffing a sigh, Brennan rolled his eyes. He fisted his hands as he put them on his hips, rolling his shoulders and hunching a little. After mumbling an apology, he glanced at Eion through his lashes.

"Well, what do I get?" Eion asked, deciding to change the subject. He had no desire to give his brother shit. However, he did make a mental note to ask his other siblings if they had any idea what was going on with Brennan.

If anyone knows, it'll be Brielle.

She and Brennan were less than a year apart. Until she'd mated years before, they'd been close.

Perhaps that's the issue. Brennan is trying to find someone to replace his relationship with our sister.

Hmmm . . .

"Well, uh . . ." Brennan's gaze darted around the area again. "Um."

His wide-eyed expression and the uncertain scent made Eion think Brennan hadn't thought that far ahead.

Good grief.

"You clean my bathroom every week for three months," Eion offered. Seeing Brennan's jaw sag open, he arched one brow imperiously. "Seems a fair bet if you want me to agree with you riding my *Harley*."

Everyone in his family knew he hated dealing with cleaning toilets.

Huffing a sigh, Brennan nodded. "Fine."

From his brother's tone, Eion knew Brennan didn't think he would lose. That was fine. He would prove him wrong.

"Very well. Have you already talked with Cliff and Niamh?" Eion asked before taking another sip of his tea.

"Yeah, they agreed," Brennan claimed, rising to his feet. He put his own glass of tea on the flat edge of an upturned cable spool that Eion used as a make-shift side table. "They said they'd meet us at the Bear Point Lake trailhead."

Eion nodded as he rose. After downing the last couple gulps of his tea, he picked up Brennan's glass and headed into his small one-bedroom cabin. His place was tucked well back in the trees. While he only owned five acres, like many of the secluded shifter homes, the plot backed up to BLM land.

After placing both glasses in the sink, Eion walked into his bedroom. He pulled on a pair of socks before returning to the front door. Sliding his feet into a pair of hiking boots, he laced them up, then straightened.

"All right then," Eion stated, exiting the cabin and closing the door securely behind him. After locking it, he shoved the keys into his pocket and smiled at his brother. "Did you text them, then?" Eion waggled his eyebrows as he gave Brennan a cheeky grin. "Ready to clean my bathroom for months?"

Brennan returned his cheek with a playful sneer. "I can't wait to enjoy driving your *Harley* through town."

Eion laughed as he headed to his quad-cab pick-up. As he climbed behind the wheel, he watched through his mirrors as Brennan jogged to his own vehicle. Once his brother had hopped inside the old *Jeep*, Eion brought his truck roaring to life.

Following Brennan, Eion looked forward to running and hunting as a wolf, especially with family. He hadn't been out in a couple of weeks. Work at Kade's mechanic shop had kept him busy.

Everyone seemed to have the same idea — *it's spring, so let's get our motorcycles tuned up, so we can ride.*

Eion had completed more oil changes and tune-ups in the last two weeks than he had in the prior month. Still, working at the fellow wolf shifter's shop made for less misunderstandings. His occasional snarl or growl didn't alarm his employer.

Hell, as an enforcer, Kade offered more than his fair share of mutterings . . . especially when he'd been away from his mate too long — a human named Tom.

When Eion reached the trailhead, he spotted both Cliff and Niamh's vehicles. His siblings were standing beside each other, chatting amicably. After parking and exiting his vehicle, Eion waved while calling a greeting.

"How'd he rope you into this?" Niamh asked, laughing good-naturedly. Her hazel eyes twinkled, and she winked. "What could he possibly have offered you for the use of your *Harley*?"

Eion shrugged as he rested his hands on his hips. "When I asked Brennan, he looked confused," he admitted with a shake of his head. Upon seeing Niamh's lifted brows, he chuckled. "So I told him when I won the hunt, he would need to clean my bathroom weekly for three months."

Niamh barked a laugh, grinning widely as she turned her attention to Brennan. "Really? You didn't come up with something before Eion made his demands?"

Brennan's cheeks took on a pinkish hue as he whipped his shirt over his head. "Come on," he demanded as he tossed it onto the seat of his *Jeep*. "Let's do this."

While they all began stripping in preparation of shifting, Cliff asked, "Do we have a time frame?" After a glance at his phone before setting it on the floorboard of Brennan's vehicle, he added, "I need to be home by eight to help Lisa put Abigail to bed."

Eion bit back a knowing smile as he exchanged a look with

Niamh. *Yep, Cliff's heart isn't gonna be in this.* His attention returned to his brothers when he heard Brennan whine, "Come on, Cliff. This is important."

In response, Cliff growled in warning. "You never did say *why* this was so important."

Spotting Brennan's annoyed glare directed at Cliff, Eion clenched his jaw. He realized there was definitely something going on with his youngest brother for him to give their pack's head tracker such a challenging look—family or not. With Lisa being pregnant, Cliff was already on edge.

Surely this isn't just about a girl.

"Let's say be back here when the sun is hanging over The Cragg," Eion cut in as he pointed to the west, reaffirming his decision to look into it later. Even from within the trees, they would be able to make out when the sun was near the cliff-face that was popular with rock climbers. "That should be about six-thirty or so, and you'll have plenty of time to get home to Lisa."

"Okay. Be back here by then," Cliff agreed.

While Brennan agreed, his expression still appeared a bit mutinous.

Oh well.

Shucking the rest of his clothes, Brennan placed everything on the floorboard of his pick-up. He nodded once to Niamh, then crouched and called to his wolf. His body immediately began to change. His skin rippled as his fur sprouted. He felt the push-pull sensation of his bones sliding and realigning within him. The pop and snap of his muscles and tendons felt like a fantastic stretch.

Eion opened his eyes and peered around. While on four paws, his perception of the world was different. His vision had grown sharper, and his nostrils were assailed with odors.

Shivering with excitement, Eion bounced forward and barreled playfully into Niamh. His sister chuffed as she snapped at him, lightly nipping his foreleg. The bite wasn't hard enough to get through his fur, but Eion growled back anyway.

Then he barked before bouncing away and pouncing on Brennan, who was rubbing against Cliff. Obviously, as a wolf, his brother wanted reassurance from the most dominant of them. For several minutes, the four wolves scuffled and played.

Finally, Cliff barked an order, and they split up to hunt. In wolf form, Eion had even less understanding of the point of the bet. Still, he was all for hunting.

Loping alongside Niamh, Eion tipped his nose into the wind, scenting the air. He caught the musky fragrance of a moose but dismissed it just as quickly. The animal was too big for just the two of them.

When Niamh slowed, her nose sniffing along the ground, Eion did the same. The pleasant odor of hare caused his mouth to water. While he didn't think the large rabbit would win the bet, it would make an enjoyable snack to fuel them for bringing down bigger game.

Eion exchanged a glance with Niamh, who tipped her muzzle toward the left, so he circled in that direction. Finding a log to hide behind, he waited, excitement pulsing through him. Tension thrummed through his body.

When the big hare bounded out from beneath the brush, bobbing and weaving, Niamh in hot pursuit, Eion judged the prey animal's next leap and lunged, landing directly in front of it. The rabbit's scent stank of fear as it jumped to the right.

Just as planned, Niamh was there to stop it. She sank her sharp teeth into the hare's neck, lifted it off the ground, and shook her head. The snap of the animal's neck could barely be heard over her aggressive growl.

Plopping onto his butt, Eion tipped his head back and howled their victory. Niamh joined him for a moment, then lowered her muzzle to the dead animal and pushed it onto its back. Utilizing her sharp canines, she tore into the animal's gut.

Eion crept forward, nosing closer, gaging his sister's receptiveness. When she tensed, he paused. Then the other wolf tore out another chunk of the belly before taking a step back to chew it.

Accepting Niamh's offer, Eion placed his paw on the rabbit's torso and sank his teeth into its haunch. He tore off a large chunk. Crunching through the meat and bone, he savored the warm, oozing flesh.

While Eion licked his chops, he watched Niamh tear off another piece of the hare.

Just when she backed away to offer him another bite, Eion paused as a new scent reached his nostrils. He whipped his head around, searching for the source. His body vibrated with excitement as heat simmered through his veins.

Niamh cocked her head as she chewed, her expression one of interest.

Unable to explain while in wolf form, Eion let out a soft whine. He rose to his feet and lifted his nose to the wind. Trotting through the forest, he stalked the source of the smell.

Vaguely, Eion saw that Niamh followed. While she carried the rest of the hare in her mouth, even in canine form, her expression betrayed her confusion.

Eion realized he recognized the area. There was a trailhead a couple of miles away, although it was rarely used. His pack liked it that way because part of the trail came a little closer to where the pack enjoyed running than they would have liked.

Slinking forward, Eion scented carefully as he followed the enticing aroma. He had his suspicions due to the way he was reacting, but he really wanted to see the object of his hunt to be certain. Anticipation thrummed through him, none-the-less.

Finally, Eion spotted a big, broad blond kneeling on a rock. He held a huge-ass rifle, resting his elbow on his upturned thigh. His focus remained on the scope, but he didn't have his finger on the trigger.

Instead, the guy appeared to be panning over the area.

To Eion's surprise, the stranger was peering in the direction of Alpha Declan's home, which was only a few miles down the steep terrain.

The intensity of the human's scent verified Eion's suspicion.

Hot damn! Finally!

Niamh recovered first, obviously jumping to the conclusion that the guy was spying on their alpha. Dropping the hare, she leaped out of the brush. She snarled and growled angrily as she stalked forward.

The human twisted and fell on his ass, shock flowing from him, sharpening his scent. The move caused his gun to swing wide, and he juggled the weapon. He muttered something in a language Eion didn't recognize, but he easily guessed he was cussing.

Not wanting his sister and the human to come to blows — or for him to be terrorized further — Eion lunged forward, following her from the thicket. As soon as his paws hit the dirt, he shifted. Pushing himself, he managed to change faster than he'd ever done before, fear for the big human's safety driving him.

"Wait," Eion panted as soon as he had a human mouth that could form words. "Niamh, please." He rocked up onto his knees and lifted his hands in placation.

While his sister had stopped growling, she still had her attention pinned on the human.

"Niamh, please," Eion said again, glancing between her and the clearly shocked, gaping human. "He's my mate."

In the next instant, the human pointed a trembling hand at him while stuttering in another tongue. Whatever he was trying to get out, he didn't manage it before he crumpled.

"Well shit," Eion muttered.

That hadn't gone as planned.

CHAPTER THREE

Like a switch being flipped — one second Castrose was asleep and the next he was awake. It had been that way ever since he could remember. No leisurely wake-ups for him.

Except, usually he recognized where he was even before he opened his eyes. Not so, this time around. Lying on a soft mattress wouldn't have been new, but feeling the heat of the sun on his face definitely was. He always closed the blinds, so no one would be able to see into the room. On top of that, the smell of pine and cleaner teased his nostrils, combining with a clearly masculine aroma.

To Castrose's surprise, the smell created a heat in his blood that caused his gut to clench and his heart beat to spike.

What the hell?

Taking all that in in an instant, Castrose kept his breathing even and slow. He feigned sleep as he listened, searching for clues even as he racked his memories for how he could have ended up there. Unfortunately, the images that came to mind caused more confusion than answers.

Castrose had been out mapping the terrain around park ranger, Declan McIntire's home. He'd found a perch a couple of miles behind the property and high enough to use his rifle's scope to view the place. The large lodge, huge back deck, and massive lawn, complete with a fire pit, had told Castrose that there was more going on than met the eye.

After all, how could a park ranger and a country doctor afford such a thing?

"I know you're awake," a soft tenor stated in English.

The Irish lilt to his words made Castrose want to hum appreciatively.

Except, what? How?

Cracking his eyelids, Castrose blinked slowly. He turned his face away from the sunlight streaming through the massive picture window to his left. After his eyes had adjusted, he peered around the room.

Castrose took in the deep forest beyond the window, telling him he was probably still in Colorado. The bedroom where he rested was quite large, with a big, comfortable, king-sized four-poster bed in dark wood tones. There were matching nightstands, a tall five-drawer dresser, as well as a lower-standing six-drawer one—those drawers were set in rows of two. The walls were a light green color, which were offset nicely by the deep green comforter pulled up to Castrose's waist.

Fabric matches the pine trees outside.

After that inane thought spun through him, Castrose realized his head hurt. He finally focused on the man sitting in a chair beside the bed. With his black eyebrows furrowed over his deep green eyes, coupled with how he leaned forward with his elbows on his knees, the handsome stranger appeared concerned.

"What happened to me?" Castrose asked.

The man cocked his head as he straightened. A confused expression creasing the corners of his lips. He rubbed the back of his neck.

"I'm sorry. I don't understand." The guy stared intently at him before speaking again, this time much more slowly. "English? Do you speak English?"

What the hell? Why is he speaking to me like a toddler?

Oh, right.

Castrose realized he'd asked in his native Swedish tongue.

Biting back an annoyed growl, Castrose tried again. "What happened to me?" Seeing the relief fill the man's eyes, making the green almost sparkle, he added, "Why does my head hurt?" Because damn, it really did. Then, realizing there was something even more pertinent, Castrose added, "Who are you?"

When the stranger smiled widely, probably pleased that they would be able to communicate, his whole face lit up. His pleasure filled his green eyes, making them twinkle. He displayed even white teeth in his deeply tanned face.

"Damn. I was worried." After that admission, he pressed his palm to his chest. "I'm Eion MacDougal. You're in my home. I live near Stone Ridge, Colorado." After a second of hesitation, Eion added, "That's in the United States."

Castrose scowled. "I know where Colorado is." His tone came out gruffer than he'd intended, but the way his body was reacting to Eion's gorgeous voice was confusing him. Castrose didn't like being confused.

He decided to focus on what he'd learned and on what he still needed to know.

So I'm still in the same area. Good.

Lifting his right hand, Castrose reached toward the back of his head. "And my head?"

To Castrose's surprise, Eion snaked his hand out whippet-fast and grabbed his wrist in a loose but firm hold. "Don't touch your head. You might tear out some stitches." His handsome features twisted into a concerned expression. "Doc would have my hide if you did that."

"Stitches," Castrose repeated slowly, although his focus slid to where Eion still touched him. The hairs on his arm lifted as goose bumps broke out over his skin. "What happened?"

"Do you remember the wolves?"

Castrose remembered them all right. He also remembered what happened after the wolf lunged for him. Surely that couldn't have actually happened, though.

Right?

Somehow, Castrose must have given his thoughts away, for Eion's smile turned warm and encouraging. He slid his hand from his wrist to his fingers, threading them together. Giving him a slight nod, Eion squeezed his hand.

"You saw something out there that overloaded your brain a bit, Castrose," Eion told him softly. "But it was true. It was all true."

"What's true?" Castrose tossed the question out there on instinct . . . and disbelief. Then something else struck him. "How do you know my name?"

Eion opened his mouth, then closed it again. His tanned cheeks took on a pinkish hue as he nibbled his bottom lip. His shoulders tensed as he rubbed the back of his neck with his free hand.

"I told him who ye were," another accented voice stated, this one deeper and full of authority.

Castrose snapped his gaze to the doorway and spotted none other than the dark-brown visage of Declan McIntire. "You," he snarled.

"Aye, and ye obviously seem to know me." Declan crossed his arms over his chest as he leaned a t-shirt-clad shoulder against the doorframe, appearing to get his broad frame comfortable. "I'd like to know how." Then Declan smirked as he added, "And how ye located us, of course."

"What did you do to my brother?" Castrose demanded, yanking his hand free of Eion's grip. "Where is Clayton?"

While roaring the question, Castrose attempted to lunge to his feet. Too bad the move caused his head to swim and his vision to gray at the edges. Only Eion's swift movement kept him from sprawling unceremoniously on the floor.

Great intimidation tactic, moron.

"Whoa, whoa, Cass," Eion cried, wrapping his arms around his torso and urging him back to the bed. "You have a concussion. You shouldn't—"

Even knowing it was a losing battle, Castrose still struggled. He swung his elbow into the smaller man's torso, aiming for his sternum. His aim was off, either due to his swimming head or how quickly Eion twisted.

Eion grunted, but his grip on Castrose's body didn't loosen. It didn't tighten, either. Instead, he insistently urged Castrose to return to his back as he whispered soothing words of encouragement into his ear.

Castrose felt his body give out, and he flopped back onto the mattress. Only Eion swiftly moving his right hand to cradle his neck kept him from hitting his head on the pillow. As it was, Castrose couldn't remember the last time his body felt so weak and uncoordinated.

"Did you give me something?" Castrose stared up at Eion, ignoring the handsome man's concerned expression. That could be the only explanation. "Meds?"

"The doc gave you a local so it was more comfortable for you while stitching your head," Eion told him, easing his grip on Castrose's neck and gently placing his head on the pillow. "But you didn't wake up. I was getting worried."

That made no sense.

"Why would you worry about me?" Castrose grimaced. That wasn't what he needed to know. "Concussion? How bad? When will I regain my coordination?"

When can I escape these people?

Although, for some reason, the idea of leaving Eion sent a sharp pang through his chest.

Odd.

Declan hummed, redrawing Castrose's attention. "Wouldn't ye want to see yer brother before ye leave?" He grinned broadly, his gray eyes twinkling. "We're not holding him against his will, ye know."

What?

"What?" Castrose voiced the thought. "That is a lie," he declared just as quickly. "If he is not being held against his will,

25

he would have contacted me. It has been almost a week."

To Castrose's surprise, Declan chuckled . . . actually chuckled. "Well." He shrugged his big shoulders as he pushed away from the wall. Grinning, he claimed, "Clayton has been distracted with all the information we've been sharing with him. I'm sure when he hears ye're here, he'll be happy to see ye."

"You will take me to him?"

Declan glanced at Eion, then met his gaze again. While shaking his head once, he pointed at the man who still hovered near his bed. "Soon, but ye need to have a conversation with Eion first." Then he arched one black brow. "Also, once we prove yer brother is alive and well, can I assume ye will not be using that rifle ye were pointing my home's way?"

Castrose glanced around quickly. "Where is my rifle?"

"Tucked away, for now," Eion told him, rubbing his shoulder soothingly. "For the safety of the pack."

"Pack?" Castrose narrowed his eyes as he watched Eion nod, his expression turning serious as he held Declan's gaze. "What does that mean?"

Eion turned his attention back to Castrose. With the way his lips appeared a bit pinched at the corners of his mouth, he appeared troubled. Still, he settled back in his chair and cleared his throat.

"Are you all part of a cult?" Castrose asked slowly. As quickly as the idea came to him, he began fitting the pieces together. As odd as it seemed, the possibility was there. "Have you done something to brain-wash my brother?"

"You have a lot of explaining to do, Eion," Declan stated, backing away. "Call me when ye're done, and I'll have Dixon bring Clayton over."

"Thank you, Alpha," Eion replied, dipping his head in what looked like a deferential move. Then he returned his focus to Castrose and stated, "No. Not a cult."

26

"I'm certain I'll be seeing quite a bit more of ye, Castrose." Declan turned and headed out of the bedroom. "Until then."

Eion sat in silence for a moment, his expression one of deep thought.

Castrose scowled as he pressed his palms to the mattress and pushed to a sitting position. He wanted answers, and he hated that he wasn't getting any. His head hurt a little, but he adjusted himself until he had his back to the headboard.

His movement must have yanked Eion out of his reverie, for he snapped his focus to him and quickly shoved a pillow behind Castrose's back, helping him.

"So, um—" Eion paused and cleared his throat. Resting his hand on Castrose's thigh, he squeezed lightly. "Right. Explanation."

Castrose felt the touch down to his toes. It also caused his groin to warm, and his mouth went dry. It was Castrose's turn to swallow. Spotting a bottle of water on the nightstand to his left, he grabbed it and twisted the cap, breaking the seal.

"Sorry," Eion murmured. "I should have offered." He tipped his chin, indicating the water.

After gulping down half the bottle, Castrose resealed the container and set it aside. He held Eion's gaze, deciding to be blunt. "What's going on here if it's not a cult? Why would my brother agree to stay?"

"That answer is two-fold," Eion began slowly, obviously choosing his words carefully. "First, this is not a cult. This is a wolf shifter pack . . . as in the race of paranormals that share their spirit with a wolf and can turn into them at will."

Eion flicked his gaze over Castrose's face, but he remained silent. Hell, what was he supposed to say to such an outlandish statement? When he just stared, Eion cleared his throat and continued.

"Next, your brother is here by choice for several reasons, or so I've heard." Eion shrugged as his smile turned shy. "I've never actually met him. I'm a tracker, like most of the people in my family, but I'm not part of the inner circle. I only help out on rare occasions." Waving his hand, Eion shook his head. "Anyway, from what Alpha Declan told me earlier, Clayton is here under the alpha's protection because an Armenian terrorist cell located your brother's whereabouts. Fortunately, we found him first, and he found our unique abilities fascinating. So—"

Lifting his hand, Castrose decided to stop the man's information dump. "Are you claiming you all are paranormal creatures that turn into wolves?" he asked, the words sounding ridiculous even as he spoke them. "Is there something wrong with your head?"

The information about the Armenians . . . well, he could check that out easily enough once he'd secured his brother. First, however, he had to get away from the crazy people.

CHAPTER FOUR

Eion sighed deeply as he took in Castrose's disbelieving expression. He should have known it wouldn't be easy. Still, his sexy handsome mate had seen him shift.

Shouldn't that have counted for something?

Wait. Maybe he doesn't remember that part. He did hit his head, after all.

"Yes, I am a paranormal being called a shifter. A wolf shifter, to be exact." Then Eion added, "I know people don't enjoy being reminded of why they fainted, but surely you remember the reason why it happened? You saw those two wolves, then one changed. That was me."

Scenting Castrose's spike of anxiety, Eion rubbed his hand up and down his mate's thigh, hoping to soothe him. He had noticed how his human's arousal had spiked when he'd first touched him, after all. Even as he felt Castrose's muscle tense, even through the fabric of the jeans he wore, Eion smelled the increase of arousal.

To Eion's pleasure, the delicious scent began to beat out the acrid smell of unease.

Nice.

"That's the way," Eion rumbled, smiling as he continued to massage the thick muscle beneath his palm. "Just relax."

Castrose's pale-blond brows furrowed as he glanced from Eion's face to where he touched him and back again. "Are you gay?"

Upon seeing Castrose's flush as his jaw sagged open, then his mouth snapped shut again, Eion chuckled softly. "I've been with males and females." Winking, he swept his gaze over his mate's large, strong-looking frame. "And you are a gorgeous specimen I hope to soon unwrap."

Once again, Castrose's jaw sagged open.

As much fun as leaning forward and capturing his shocked mate's lips would have been, Eion knew it wasn't the time . . . yet. Instead, he winked before refocusing on the explanations. "So, do you remember seeing me shift before passing out?"

"Y-You're claiming" — pausing, Castrose swallowed hard enough to cause his Adam's apple to bob — "that one of the wolves was you?"

Eion nodded. "Exactly. I shifted to stop my sister from injuring you." He grimaced as he settled a hard look Castrose's way. "You were pointing a sniper rifle at our alpha's home, you recall."

"My finger wasn't on the trigger. I was —" Growling, Castrose glared at him. "Seriously? That's what I'm focusing on? I *must* be concussed." Rubbing at his forehead, he cast a side-eyed gaze Eion's way before grumbling, "You're hitting on me, touching me, and my dick is hard, even though you just told me I really did see a wolf turn into a man, and it was you. What the fuck is wrong with me?"

Giving Castrose a cheeky smile, Eion waggled his eyebrows. "Well, part of being a paranormal is the fact that Fate grants us a mate. A soul mate." Upon seeing his human's eyes narrowing, he hurried to explain, "A shifter lives a hell of a long time, Cass. Upwards of five hundred years." Eion leaned a little closer, silently willing Castrose to accept, to believe. "When we recognize our mate, which we do by scent, we pursue that person and bond with him or her. In the case of a human, it will extend their life to match mine."

Eion paused and waited, wondering how his mate would respond.

For a long moment, Castrose just stared . . . as if waiting for more information. He began to reach for the back of his head again, as if intending to rub at his wound. Evidently catching himself, he heaved a sigh and returned his hand to his lap.

"You still haven't told me what that has to do with me."

Upon hearing Castrose's softly rumbled comment, Eion gaped. He had thought that would have been self-explanatory, but it seemed he would have to spell it out. Moving his hand from his mate's thigh, he took Castrose's left hand between both of his own, threading their fingers together. Eion leveled a serious look his human's way as he stated, "Castrose, I have been waiting for you over a hundred years. *You* are my mate, and the attraction between us is part of that." Hoping what he said next wouldn't send the big human running, Eion explained, "Fate has a way of ramping up the attraction between mates, encouraging us to complete the bond as swiftly as possible."

Licking his lips, Castrose furrowed his brows and narrowed his eyes. His expression turned a little vacant. "Can any of this actually be real?" He whispered the words, almost as if he were trying to sort through all the information that Eion had shared.

"It is real," Eion confirmed quietly, massaging the back of Castrose's hand with his thumb. "I know it's a reality shift, but please believe me when I say it's not a bad change."

Castrose blinked twice, then focused on Eion. He swept his gaze over his chest, then up to his face. Meeting his gaze, he cocked his head.

"Why would you tell me any of this?" Castrose peered at him with an incredulous look. "Shouldn't you be guarding this secret? I mean, don't you all worry about persecution or something?"

"We do, and normally, we guard the secret jealously." Eion brought Castrose's hand to his lips, and he pressed a kiss to his palm. To his pleasure, his human didn't resist, and he hoped that meant he was drawing strength from his touch. "I am telling you for two reasons. One, your brother is here, and he knows. The bigger reason, however" — he hesitated a second, realizing he didn't know a damn thing about his mate — *still* —"is because you are my mate and need to know these things in order to understand our way of life."

Castrose sighed deeply as he stared at where Eion massaged his hand. "This could be a dream or hallucination brought on by my concussion."

"It's not," Eion countered, shaking his head, frustration slipping through him. Huffing a sigh, he frowned at the man. "You're going to be a stubborn one, aren't you?"

"I don't believe the crazy tale you're spinning, and I'm being stubborn?" Castrose smiled widely, laughing softly as he shook his head. "For all I know I'll wake up in an hour and realize this has all been a dream."

Eion sighed again. "Okay. You go ahead and believe that then." Squeezing Castrose's hand once more before releasing it, he offered his human a rakish grin. "If time is what you need, then that's what you'll have. After all, we'll have centuries together."

Castrose barked a laugh, disbelief lighting his clear blue eyes. Then he winced and lifted his free hand to his temple.

"Careful," Eion admonished gently. "Head injury. Remember?"

As Castrose fingered around the edge of the bandage, Eion heard his human's stomach rumbling. Humming, he rose to his feet. "The doc ordered you to stay in bed, but I bet you're hungry. He said something light would be okay."

"Who is this doc you keep talking about?" Then Castrose's eyes widened as he glanced toward the doorway. "Do you mean Doctor Lark Trystan? Declan's partner?"

"I do." Eion released Castrose and headed toward the door. "How about grilled cheese and tomato soup?" Pausing in the doorway, he peered back at his mate. "Would that work? Or are you allergic to something?"

"Allergic to shellfish."

Eion nodded. "All shellfish?"

Castrose grunted. "Oysters, clams, shrimp, lobster." He rolled one shoulder in a half-shrug. "They make my throat close up and my lips swell."

"Damn!" Eion mumbled, wincing. "That sucks. Duly noted." Humming as he turned away, he wondered out loud, "I wonder if that will change after we bond."

"Wait a minute."

Eion paused again and turned back to face Castrose. He swept his gaze over his reclining form, admiring his broad shoulders, narrow hips, and thickly muscled limbs. His blood heated as his heart rate sped up.

Gods, my mate in my bed is a thing of beauty.

When Eion had shifted to stop Niamh from biting Castrose to take his gun away, he'd been so focused on the exquisite scent of the man that he hadn't taken the time to notice his human's body. Even after, other things had distracted him. First, there'd been the bleeding head wound caused by Castrose striking his head against the side of a sharp rock when he'd fainted. After that, Eion had been too focused on getting his injured mate into his home as well as getting him aid. Finally, when Alpha Declan and his mate, Lark, had arrived, Eion had learned that the pair knew who Castrose was.

Eion had been dealing with one thing after another—finding his mate, securing his safety, and now explaining shifters and the paranormal. He hadn't had the time just to admire the male specimen that Fate had deemed his soul mate.

And gods, what a specimen.

Even reclining, Eion could see that Castrose stood six-foot-three. His skin appeared fair with pale blond hairs smattering over his muscular limbs. Even his strong-looking hands caused Eion's skin to tingle with his need to feel the calloused digits on his skin.

Groaning under his breath, Eion reached down and adjusted himself.

"Eion?"

Upon hearing his name in Castrose's accented tone, Eion shook himself. He returned his focus to his mate's face, only to find his human staring at his groin. Eion cleared his throat as he released his crotch, since he'd still been cupping himself from when he'd shifted his hard dick.

Eion felt his cheeks heat, but he did his best to ignore the reaction. After all, he found his mate hot. Over the years, he bet he would be springing a boner for him often.

"I'm sorry. What?" Eion asked, trying to bring Castrose's attention back to whatever had caused the man to call his name. His mate had asked him to pause before preparing food, after all. "Did you need something else first? Aspirin or something?"

Wait. Can Castrose have aspirin with a head injury?

Eion realized he would have to call the alpha-mate if that ended up being Castrose's request.

"You said *when* we bond."

Focusing around his arousal was damn tough. Eion couldn't remember anyone telling him about that particular side-effect of finding his mate. Analyzing his human's comment, he couldn't find a question in there.

Still, Eion nodded in confirmation. "I did."

"Like it's a foregone conclusion." Castrose's eyes narrowed as he peered at him with a serious gaze. "And you're hard as a rock thinking about it."

Eion glanced at his fly, which bulged blatantly. Meeting Castrose's gaze again, he shrugged. "You're a big sexy man. Is it any wonder I find you so attractive?"

"You don't know anything about me."

"True." Eion had heard that humans often had that particular hang-up. "We don't currently know anything about each other, but that will change in time."

"But isn't bonding permanent?" Castrose rubbed his hands over his thighs, betraying his unease. "The way you talked, that's the impression I got."

"Yes, bonding is permanent," Eion confirmed. He really had missed a few things. Not surprising, since there was a lot to explain. "You will be mine, and I will be yours." Growling upon seeing Castrose begin to shake his head, Eion quickly added, "And there will be no chance of straying. I won't even get it up for another, and if another dares to touch you—" He growled, clenching his hands.

Castrose appeared to understand his meaning, for he quickly stated, "Got it." He even lifted a hand in placation. "Your kind are jealous, then."

"Of our fated bonded mate? Hell yeah." Eion began to turn, needing a moment to gather himself and calm down. Glancing over his shoulder, he added, "Some of us wait centuries. Remember?" Then Eion headed to his kitchen.

Eion made quick work of pulling out the needed ingredients. After scooping some bacon fat into a frying pan to melt, he began slathering the bread with butter. Slicing some medium cheddar cheese, Eion debated adding a bit of turkey meat to them.

Deciding against it, Eion stacked two sandwiches into the prepared pan, then pulled out a plastic container from the refrigerator. He opened it and poured the contents—homemade tomato soup he'd made three days prior—into a pot. Turning the burner on medium heat, Eion hummed as he pinched the corner of the bread and checked the progress of the sandwich.

Not surprising, the butter had just melted. Since Eion had the pan on low heat, he knew it would be a couple of minutes until it began to brown. That was how he liked it. The longer, slower cook time meant the cheese had ample time to melt into tasty gooiness.

Yum!

While the first two sandwiches cooked, Eion prepared a second set. He didn't know how large of an appetite his big mate had, yet. Hell, it was possible he wouldn't even be able to enjoy the solid food.

With that thought in mind, Eion turned his attention to the tomato soup, stirring the warming concoction slowly. He loved tomato soup after a run in wolf form. His brothers thought him crazy for it.

Thinking about the run that had been interrupted reminded Eion of the bet. He winced, worried about his *Harley*. Due to finding his mate, Eion had forfeited.

Niamh and Cliff had tried to convince Brennan that it wasn't a fair win, but his youngest brother had insisted.

Eion had acquiesced.

Finding my mate is worth any price . . . even if Brennan wrecks my bike.

Making a mental note to give his motorcycle a once-over after Castrose fell asleep, Eion grated some cheese to sprinkle on top of the soup. He wanted his bike to be in good working order, which would give his brother the optimal chance of returning it safely to him. Eion really wished he had more faith in his brother . . . but he knew better.

Sighing deeply, Eion flipped the sandwiches before pulling out plates and bowls. The scent of the food tantalized his senses, and his mouth watered. He allowed the tasty smells to distract him from his thoughts for a few minutes as he finished up the light meal.

CHAPTER FIVE

After the meal, which Castrose had found delicious, he spent the time dozing and trying to wrap his mind around everything Eion had told him. Due to his concussion, his handsome attendant woke him every hour. He would chat with him for a few minutes, making certain his head was clear, then leave him to rest.

Castrose found his gaze sliding to Eion's ass each and every time he left the room. As crazy as all the information the man had given him was, he couldn't deny his attraction to the guy. The way Eion woke him each time didn't help — sliding his palms along his arms, up his neck, and over his head.

Never had Castrose felt someone touch him so sensually, with so much obvious desire. Eion's green eyes gleamed with hunger, and his lips curved into a wicked smile. The way the odd man continually glanced at Castrose's lips told him he wanted to kiss him.

That knowledge unsettled Castrose a little. Even as his stomach muscles fluttered under Eion's gentle ministrations, his heart thundered in his chest. Castrose had never kissed a man before.

What would it be like?

Having always hooked up with men in clubs, Castrose had never given it much thought. He'd never even been tempted. The idea of making out with a twink who he chose to speak with only to have him suck his dick certainly didn't appeal.

Is this part of the weird mate-thing that Eion had spoken of?

Castrose wondered if he could ask. Eion had always been straight with him before. Besides, it was damn obvious that the lithe, toned, black-haired man wanted to do the same.

With so many thoughts swirling through his brain, Castrose struggled to shut down his mind and find sleep, even though Eion had told him it had been long enough to where he was no longer in danger of his concussion. The stars and a crescent moon shown through the window and had been for hours. His eyesight had long since adjusted, allowing him to make out everything in the room with ease. He had heard Eion puttering around somewhere beyond the bedroom door, but now all was silent.

Could I escape? If I did, where would I go? These men are supposed to bring my brother to me, though.

Castrose couldn't decide what to do. Easing to a sitting position, he reached for the water on the nightstand, only to find the bottle empty. Sighing, he shoved off the covers and stared down at his sweatpants-covered legs.

Eion had been kind enough to give him a pair of his sweats, so he didn't have to sleep in his jeans. When he'd offered to help him change, Castrose had shaken his head. Then he'd had to admit that he didn't wear underwear.

After leering at him and staring pointedly at his crotch, Eion had stated, "Ah, a man after my own heart." As he'd spoken, he'd rubbed his palm over his stomach, then down to his fly.

Once again, Castrose's attention had been drawn to Eion's large bulge.

One thing could be said for the sexy fucker, he was well hung, if that lump was anything to go by.

Easing to his feet, Castrose felt relief when his head didn't swim. He still had a slight residual sting to the right side at the back of it where he knew the stitches were, but that would fade in time. Castrose couldn't remember the last time his bell had been rung so badly.

Castrose padded barefoot to the door and eased it open the rest of the way. The hall only went in one direction, stretching thirty feet. There was a door on the left and two doors on the right. The one on the left was closed, but the first one on the right stood open.

As Castrose drew near it, he saw it was a large bathroom. There was a massive jetted tub, a huge slate-covered shower complete with a seat and rain-shower head. There was also a double vanity with plenty of counter space. Spotting a door to the left of a huge cupboard, he guessed that would be the water closet.

His bladder twinged.

Huh.

Closing himself into the room, Castrose quickly used the facilities. He washed up, splashing water on his face. After drying off, he returned to his exploration of the home.

The door across from the bathroom opened silently under Castrose's hand. He'd expected a second bedroom. Instead, he found a library and office combo. Two walls were covered in floor to ceiling bookshelves. There was a window seat covered in comfortable pillows and blankets, and Castrose suddenly found himself imagining Eion curling up there with a book. In the middle of the room was a small desk with a closed laptop and a lamp sitting on it.

Backing out of the room, Castrose closed the door. When he opened the final door, he discovered a linen and storage closet. Having reached the end of the hall, Castrose peered around.

This section of the home had an open-floor concept. To the right was a spacious kitchen with a bar that separated it from the dining room. He saw a massive living space, complete with an L-shaped sectional, a reclining chair, a big flatscreen hanging on a wall, and matching coffee and side table.

"Something you need, handsome?"

Upon hearing Eion's soft voice, Castrose snapped his gaze

back to the sectional. Bare-chested, his hands behind his head, the handsome man reclined on the cushions from where he stared at him. He sported a wide grin as he waggled his brows at Castrose.

"Uh—"

Real eloquent, bub.

"Can't sleep?" Eion sat up, shoving off the blanket that had been pulled to his waist in the process. "Need something to drink? Eat?" Smirking, Eion rose to his feet as he began sauntering toward him. "Or were you intending to run out the door in the middle of the night?"

Castrose found his gaze straying to the darker man's bare torso and the light smattering of chest hair there. His fingers twitched with his desire to touch. Feeling his blood heat and flow south, he swallowed hard and forced his focus back to Eion's face.

That didn't help much, since the heat in the man's expression and the appreciative gleam in his eyes made it clear where his thoughts were.

"W-Water," Castrose finally managed to rasp. He cleared his throat and tried again. "Was going to get a glass of water."

The way Eion arched his brow told Castrose that he didn't believe him. "All right." He drew close and rested his hand on his shoulder, causing the skin of his upper arms to goose bump. "I know you've been dozing most of the day. Having trouble sleeping?"

Using his warm hold, Eion urged Castrose to turn. Then he removed his hand, and Castrose felt the loss of it, immediately wanting his touch back again. Before he could analyze the odd feeling, Eion placed his hand on his lower back and pushed lightly.

Castrose waffled between the urge to pull away and push back into the slightly shorter, slenderer man's touch. "Why am I liking your touch so much?" The words were out of his mouth before he could think better of them.

"Because you're my mate." Eion rubbed his thumb over his spine as he walked beside him. "You will always enjoy my touch." They reached a barstool, and Eion murmured, "Have a seat. Are you hungry, too? Dinner was hours ago."

"Uh—" Castrose's knee-jerk reaction was to say no. *Except* — "Is there more of that soup? No way is that canned shit. Where did you get it?"

Eion appeared extremely pleased as he rubbed his hand up Castrose's spine and over his shoulder as he rounded the counter. Then he moved into the kitchen. First, he grabbed a glass from the drying rack and filled it from the dispenser on the refrigerator door.

As Eion placed it on the counter before Castrose, he told him, "Nope. Definitely not canned shit." He winked as he returned to the fridge, opening it. "And, yep. I have more." He pulled out a container, then a block of cheese. "I'll heat us some. Do you want another sandwich, too?"

Castrose shook his head. "Not this late, but thank you." It was damn tempting, though. "It was truly delicious, however. Perfectly toasted with a hint of something else." Watching Eion start dolloping some of the soup into a pot that he had also pulled from the drying rack, Castrose leaned forward and rested his forearms on the counter as he cupped his water glass between his palms. "Care to tell me what that was?"

Glancing over his shoulder at him, Eion hummed. His brows were furrowed, and he appeared in thought. "Huh. Nothing special." He carried a plate, the grater, and the block cheese to the counter between them. As he shredded some mild cheddar, he continued, "Medium cheddar thinly sliced. Buttered bread. Although it is homemade." He pointed over his shoulder at the soup. "So's that. I like to cook." Then he snapped his attention back to Castrose and added, "Maybe it's because I grill it in bacon grease?"

Castrose nodded absently, processing that. "Bacon grease and homemade bread," he mused softly. "Wow, you make your own bread?"

He couldn't think of anyone else he knew that did that.

Eion nodded, his cheeks taking on a pinkish hue as he muttered, "I find cooking and baking relaxing." Clearing his throat, he added, "Besides, as a wolf shifter, I have a big appetite. By cooking my own food from scratch, I can make extra-large sizes, giving me plenty of leftovers for later." While brushing off the cheese grater, Eion met his gaze. "On top of that, processed food has so much shit in it. I like knowing what's actually in my food."

Having never looked at it that way, Castrose nodded. "Okay." He ignored the wolf shifter comment, since he still wasn't certain he believed that. Instead, Castrose complimented, "Well, your soup and sandwiches were certainly fantastic."

"Thanks." Eion winked and grinned at him as he moved back to the soup so he could stir it. "You'll never go hungry. That's for sure."

Castrose nodded absently before he recognized the insinuation in Eion's words. He would never go hungry because he was staying there with him. Eion obviously expected him to accept the shifter and bonding thing.

"Are we attracted to each other only because of this mate thing you believe in?" Castrose had asked something similar before, but he hadn't received a definitive answer.

"Yes and no."

Yep, that isn't an answer, either.

Sighing deeply, Castrose scowled at Eion. "It can't be both."

Eion poured the soup into two bowls, then sprinkled cheese over each. After picking them up, he rounded the counter. He placed one bowl in front of Castrose before placing the second in front of the stool to his left. Finally, Eion grabbed two spoons and returned once more.

After handing Castrose one spoon, Eion settled on the stool beside him. "Yes, the heightened attraction between us is in part due to the fact that we're mates." Eion leaned on his elbow, turning to stare intently at Castrose. "No, we would have been attracted to each other anyway."

Castrose slid his spoon into the soup, unable to resist the allure of the tasty-smelling fluid. "How do you know that?" he asked before easing the flavorful liquid into his mouth. He hummed appreciatively as the rich tomato soup with a bit of mild cheddar burst across his taste buds. "So good," Castrose murmured before eagerly taking another bite.

Eion chuckled softly, clearly pleased at Castrose's enjoyment. "Think of it this way," he began before taking a sip of his own soup. He hummed and swallowed, then told him, "We spot each other across a crowded room. You think I'm pretty hot, but there's a lot of people, and getting through them all would be a pain in the ass." Snickering, Eion winked as he took another spoonful. "Normally, you wouldn't bother." He waved his spoon in the air dismissively. "After all, there are always plenty of fish in the sea."

Then Eion's expression grew serious as he pinned a heated look on Castrose. "What Fate does is give you that extra burst of attraction that acts as incentive to make your way across the crowded room to talk to me." Resting his free hand on Castrose's thigh, he squeezed lightly. "The rest is up to us to make it work." His tone turned husky as Eion gave him a heated look. "And I do want to make it work."

Goose bumps broke out on the skin of Castrose's leg, and he felt his muscles jump beneath Eion's palm. His blood heated, and his breath caught in his throat. Even his nipples beaded . . . and all from a gentle caress and a hungry look.

Holy shit.

Castrose found himself nodding without any conscious thought on his part. His body seemed to be responding all on its own. Shifting uncomfortably in his seat, he spread his legs a little to make room for his thickening dick.

"Gods, how you respond to me is—" Eion groaned as he squeezed Castrose's thigh a bit harder. "Eat your soup, Cass. Then I'm gonna suck your dick."

Moaning gruffly, Castrose returned to eating, but focusing on it was damn tough. His hand began to tremble as he felt Eion slid his hand to the inside of his leg. He scraped his fingernails over the inseam, teasing at his sensitive flesh.

All the while, Eion somehow managed to continue eating sedately.

Cock-teasing fucker.

Castrose growled under his breath.

Two can play at this game.

Putting down his spoon, Castrose cradled his soup bowl in both hands. He lifted it to his lips and tipped it, drinking deeply. As much as Castrose enjoyed the taste, he would savor the soup another time.

He needed something other than food right then.

Castrose returned the bowl to the counter when it was nearly empty. He spotted Eion's lifted brow and amused expression as he picked up his spoon. Smirking back at the man, Castrose used the utensil to scoop up the last of the cheese and soup and quickly ate it.

"So glad you like it," Eion stated with a grin before eating another spoonful of his own still half-full bowl.

"I do like it. A lot." Castrose couldn't help the soft growl filling his voice. His throbbing dick called for attention, sending need coursing through him. "But there's something else I would like even more."

"And what would that be?" Eion's voice came out husky, and he slid his palm down to tease at the inside of his knee.

Castrose saw the way Eion lifted his left brow in silent challenge. "This."

Using his feet on the stool's rungs for purchase, Castrose

lifted his hips. At the same time, he gripped the hem of his sweatpants and shoved them down just enough to free his aching cock and swollen balls. Castrose gripped his dick in his right hand as he cupped his testicles with his left.

Eion gasped. His jaw sagged open, and his hand on Castrose's knee tightened. His bare chest heaved as he riveted his gaze on Castrose's groin.

Oh yeah.

Tugging gently on his erection, Castrose caressed his sensitive length. He used his thumb to roll his foreskin over his crown, spreading his pre-cum and offering teasing views of his slit. All the while, he gently squeezed and relaxed the fingers of his left hand, stimulating his balls.

"Oh fuck me," Eion whispered, his Adam's apple bobbing as he swallowed hard.

"I would be happy to."

Eion's green eyes sparkled in the dim illumination given off by only the stove light. When Eion lifted his gaze and peered at Castrose, he licked his lips. Hot desire burned within their depths.

"I sure hope you're a switch," Eion whispered as he dropped the spoon on the counter. He slid from his stool and sank to his knees, grinning up at Castrose. "Because I plan to fuck you, too, my mate."

Castrose had never bottomed in his life. His asshole clenched, and he opened his mouth to say no. Except, then Eion stuck out his tongue and licked over his crown, teasing under his foreskin. Instead, he let out his breath in a harsh gasp.

Grinning up at Castrose, Eion gripped his wrists and tugged, pulling his hands away from himself. "Grab the edge of your seat," Eion ordered in a low, gruff voice. Waggling his brows, he added, "I wouldn't want you falling off."

"Think you're that good, huh?" Castrose replied gruffly, but he still obeyed.

"I'm gonna make you shoot so damn quick, Castrose," Eion vowed as he reached for the waistband of his sweats. He tugged them down and off, then pushed Castrose's thighs wider.

Castrose sucked in a harsh breath, suddenly feeling exposed. As Eion positioned himself between Castrose's thighs, skimming his palms up his inner thighs, his cock didn't seem to care, twitching where it jutted from his groin. Swallowing hard, Castrose waited with bated breath as Eion leaned over and opened his mouth.

When Eion wrapped his lips around Castrose's crown and gave it that first light suckle, all concern about his position fled as pleasure shot through his groin.

"Oh, fuck yeah," Castrose muttered, a tremble working through him. The vision of Eion on his knees before him, between his legs, suddenly became the sexiest fucking thing he'd ever seen. "Suck me."

Eion peered at him beneath long lashes and did exactly that, causing Castrose's balls to roll and his cock to throb in the most delicious of ways.

CHAPTER SIX

Reveling in each and every moan, grunt, and hiss escaping Castrose's throat, Eion focused on the thick erection parting his lips. On each upstroke, he teased at his frenulum before sweeping his tongue over his crown, pushing at the foreskin. Then Eion sank down on Castrose's shaft, rubbing down the thick vein running the length. He lodged the crown in his throat and swallowed around the leaking knob. Then he started the whole process over again, sucking hard as he returned to Castrose's head.

Eion gripped Castrose's hip firmly with his left hand as his mate's body gave an especially hard jerk. While his human had his hands wrapped around the edge of the stool in a white-knuckled grip, he didn't want to chance his man falling. He'd already had one head injury, after all.

Cradling Castrose's balls with his right hand, Eion got a feel for his sensitivity. The way his human shuddered and trembled every time he lifted the sack a little and rolled the orbs within caused a rush of smugness, making his own groin tingle. When Eion skimmed his fingertips behind his balls and rubbed lightly over his prostate from the outside, Castrose roared his pleasure. His mate's prick swelled just a little more before a burst of seed shot down his throat.

Easing off just a little, Eion allowed the next shot to land on his tongue. He moaned as the slightly bitter tasty goodness hit his taste buds, and he hummed appreciatively at the delicious taste. As Eion continued to suck and lick on Castrose's pulsing cock, he teased his fingertips down even further, feathering his touch over his mate's hole.

Even out of his mind with lust, Eion didn't miss the way Castrose tensed even as his dick spurted one more burst. His mate growled, the sound one of clear warning. Eion didn't penetrate his human, but he didn't remove his finger either.

Instead, Eion just continued to tease at the tight muscle.

I'll get him used to the idea.

His wolf would accept no less until he'd fully claimed his man.

Eion gently eased off Castrose's prick, licking along the length like a lollipop. As he peered at his mate through his lashes, taking in his flushed cheeks, heavy-lidded gaze, and slightly parted lips, pride flooded him at putting such a debauched look on his face. After placing a kiss to the tip of Castrose's foreskin, Eion offered his new — and final — lover a cheeky smile.

"Is that what you needed, my mate?" Eion crooned, his voice a little raspy from sucking his mate's dick. He continued to tease at Castrose's hole. "Or do you want another couple of orgasms?"

Castrose's eyes narrowed as his nostrils flared. His chest heaved as he glanced down where Eion continued to tease him. Meeting his gaze again, he clenched his jaw for an instant.

While Castrose seemed to be thinking about it, his dick began to firm right back up.

"A-Another?" Castrose's thighs tensed, and he shifted a little on the stool. "Too old for that."

"Not at all, my handsome sexy mate," Eion countered, grinning widely. "If I opened you up and drilled into your prostate over and over, you would come all over us." He couldn't help but shift his gaze to the pulsing vein running up the length of Castrose's neck. His mouth watered as he anticipated sinking his canines into it and drinking deeply, bonding them for eternity. "Then when I sink my canines into your flesh, sealing our bond, the pleasure will be so great that you'll come all over again."

Castrose slowly released the stool. He gripped Eion's wrist with his left hand and gently pulled his fingers away from his anus. His expression became unreadable.

"You're talking about shit I don't believe in, yet," Castrose rumbled softly as he moved Eion's hand to his own thigh. "Stand up," he ordered. As soon as he rose to his feet, Castrose slid his fingertips into the waistband of Eion's lounging pants and eased them down. "And I never bottomed before. Don't know if I wanna."

Eion hissed upon feeling Castrose's long, thick fingers wrap around his newly freed erection. Glancing between his mate's face and his hand, he rested his hands on Castrose's shoulders. He bucked his hips, groaning at the pleasant feel of his human's callouses sliding along his shaft.

"Fuck, don't stop," Eion urged, bucking his hips. He'd been damn close just at the taste of his mate's flesh, pre-cum, and seed. "So good."

Castrose cupped Eion's balls as he sped up his hand jacking his shaft. "God, you're sexy, Eion," he muttered, his gaze raking over Eion's body like a physical caress. "I can feel how tight your balls are. You wanna come, don't you? Wanna paint my belly with your seed."

"Yessss," Eion hissed. If he couldn't claim his mate, yet, marking him with his scent was the next best thing. "Gonna make you smell like mine," he snarled, tightening his hold on Castrose's shoulders, rutting swiftly into his mate's tight grip. "Everyone will know you're taken."

Well, the paranormals will, anyway.

Eion knew that, even after a shower, his scent would still cling to Castrose's skin. That thought, coupled with the exquisite hold his mate had on his genitals, sent him flying over the edge. His balls pulled tight to his body as a flush of heat spread out through his groin. Eion moaned wantonly as he watched his cock pulse, expelling his seed all over Castrose's chest, stomach, and groin.

"Cass," Eion ground out through gritted teeth as his mate continued to stroke him, extending his bliss.

"That all you have for me?" Castrose teased as he gentled his hold and slowed his movements.

Eion chuffed a laugh as he grinned at where Castrose continued to tease him. "You keep that up, and I won't soften." Releasing his left hand's hold on his mate's shoulder, he crooked his forefingers. He then skimmed them up the underside of Castrose's half-hard dick as he murmured, "Then I'll tease you back to arousal, take you back to my bed, and sixty-nine us. You wanna suck my cock, Cass?"

Castrose's eyes narrowed. For an instant, he stopped his motions. Then he licked his lips as he started moving his hands again, but slower.

"Never done that, either," Castrose admitted softly. Holding Eion's gaze, he continued on a murmur, "You may not want to bother trying to mate with me. I may be a disappointment."

Eion cocked his head as he continued to fondle Castrose's shaft with a soft touch. "You are my mate, Castrose," he crooned, hoping to soothe the sudden bout of nerves pouring off his lover. "You could never be a disappointment. If there's something you wish to learn, I will teach you." Then Eion waggled his brows. "I've been around for over a century, so I've tried a number of things. But if we hit on something I haven't done, I look forward to exploring it with you."

Castrose licked his lips again, his gaze falling to Eion's swollen shaft again. "God, you weren't kidding," he whispered. "You're still hard." Then he moaned and shifted in his seat. "And you're making me hard, too. Fuck! How is this possible?"

Hearing the whine in Castrose's voice pulled a chuckle

from Eion. "I'm a paranormal, Castrose, and we have a higher sex drive on a normal day." He continued to tease his human's erection to full arousal as he spoke. "But right now, I'm in front of my unbonded mate. My sexy, naked unbonded mate." Eion groaned as he admired Castrose's body with a slow, thorough once, twice-over before he returned his focus to his man's ice-blue eyes. "And you respond to me because of pretty much the same reasons. Your libido will be boosted until we seal the deal, so to speak."

Castrose scowled at him. "So you're saying that you're manipulating my body's pheromones or something?" He stopped stroking Eion, but he didn't release him—*thank the gods.* Then Castrose asked, "If I walked away and never saw you again, would my arousal return to normal?"

Eion growled low in his throat. His wolf seconded that, rumbling in his mind. "Don't fucking say that," he demanded, stepping forward and pushing into Castrose's space. "I've been waiting a long damn time for you, Cass, and if you try to leave now, I will hunt you down. Get me?"

As much as Eion hated practically threatening Castrose, there was no way in hell he would allow his mate to leave now. Castrose was his, and the sooner the big lug accepted that fact, the sooner they could start their lives together. Eion just had to figure out a way to make him accept that.

Castrose's cheeks flushed, and his acrid scent told Eion it was for a reason other than arousal. Anger perfumed the air. Releasing Eion's balls, Castrose gripped his upper arm instead . . . and squeezed.

"Are you threatening me, Eion?" Castrose snarled, fury sparked in his blue eyes, somehow managing to make them appear like ice chips. "Because that wouldn't be too smart."

Okay, maybe I should have used different wording.

Seeing as they hardly knew each other, misunderstandings were bound to happen. It was inevitable.

We just need to work on our communication.

51

Releasing Castrose's dick, Eion lifted his arms . . . slowly. The move dislodged his mate's hand from his bicep, pleasing him that he wasn't staying his movements. Finally, Eion rested his forearms over Castrose's shoulders.

Eion cradled Castrose's neck with one hand and his skull with the other, teasing his fingertips through his hair. "I'm not threatening you," he purred softly. "I'm sharing my nature with you." Quirking his left lip up, Eion added, "I know you don't yet believe in the paranormal, but I have to be honest if we're going to make a relationship work."

To Eion's relief, the tension in Castrose's shoulders eased as did the scent of anger filling the air. "Relationship? Already?" Growling low in his throat, he rested his hands on Eion's hips as he muttered, "Aren't you jumping the gun, as the saying goes?"

"I'm a shifter who's found his mate. We *do* do things fast," Eion confirmed, nodding. "Our animal instinct demands it."

Sliding forward, Eion removed the last bit of space between them, flushing their bodies together. He barely suppressed a shiver upon feeling his human's bigger, broader, hard body pressed against his own from groin to nipple. The warmth of Castrose's skin against Eion's own caused his erection to twitch where it was pressed against his mate's.

"After meeting our mate, a shifter's instinct drives us to focus on a few things."

Eion struggled to explain, but with the feel of his mate against him and the smells of their mingled releases, he found it damn difficult to think. How Castrose's thumbs felt skimming along his hip bones only made it more difficult.

Taking a shuddering breath, Eion forced words out of his mouth. "I need to see to your safety, happiness, and pleasure." When Castrose's brows lifted, he quickly told him, "I can't do that if you're not near." Unable to help himself, Eion leaned his head forward and brushed his lips against the corner of his mate's. "Safe." Rubbing his cheek against Castrose's, he nuzzled his human, rubbing their scents together. "Happy." Then he skimmed sucking wet kisses down his lover's jaw to his neck, his mouth watering with his need to take a bite. His words came out garbled as he mumbled, "And well pleasured. *Well* pleasured."

Then Castrose tipped his head, offering him more room, and Eion moaned against his flesh.

"You want me well pleasured?" Castrose rumbled, his throat muscles bobbing against Eion's lips. As he spoke, he slid his hands around and gripped Eion's ass. "How well pleasured?" Castrose used the hold to rock Eion's hips forward and back while massaging his cheeks.

Eion moaned at the stimulation. Not only was his mate allowing him to work up a mark on his neck as he sucked and licked the lightly salted flesh, but his dick slid between their sweat-slicked bodies, rubbing and sliding against Castrose's answering erection. The way his mate dug his fingertips into his trench and skimmed along the sensitive intimate flesh caused a shudder to rack through him.

Wait. Didn't he ask me something? Right.

"Any pleasure you wish," Eion rumbled, lifting his head to meet Castrose's gaze as he continued to rock in his human's hold. "I am yours. Tell me, and it will be done."

Castrose's blue eyes glimmered in the dim lighting as a feral smile curved his full lips. "I want in here," he stated bluntly as he rubbed a fingertip over Eion's hole. "Tell me I can fuck you, Eion."

Moaning, Eion pressed back into Castrose's touch. "If that's what you want" — he grinned and hissed when he felt his mate's thick finger breach his muscle — "I'll happily let you mount me."

As Castrose sank his digit deeper, Eion clenched rhythmically on it.

In response, Castrose groaned, and his eyelids went heavy-lidded.

Needing a taste of that, Eion didn't think twice. He leaned forward and sealed his lips over Castrose's. Feeling his mate gasp, Eion took complete advantage. He thrust in his tongue, delving deep, ravishing and tasting the heavenly goodness that was his human.

CHAPTER SEVEN

When Eion first sank his tongue into Castrose's mouth, he'd frozen. He'd never kissed anyone before, had never wanted to or seen the allure. As he felt the teasing glide of Eion's tongue and tasted the other man, he was yanked out of his shock damn fast.

Pleasant tingles erupted on his neck, shooting down his chest. The hairs on the back of his neck stood on end, and his nipples beaded. Even his gut clenched spastically as Eion continued to ply his mouth with his tongue.

Oh damn!

Castrose began reciprocating, sliding his tongue against Eion's. The smooth rub intensified the sensations racking his body. Needing more, he lifted his left hand and cradled Eion's skull. Castrose tightened his right hand, easing his middle finger deeper into the smaller man's tight channel.

Feeling Eion's chute muscles milk his digit, Castrose moaned. He pushed his finger in as deep as he could as he squeezed the man tighter against his chest. Gripping the other man's black hair, Castrose forced him to tip his head back so he could plunge his tongue deeper.

Even though Castrose had his legs spread, he felt powerful, in control. He huffed noisily as he lapped along Eion's teeth and mapped his mouth. His cock throbbed as he used his hold to rock the other man's dick against his own.

To Castrose's shock, his body flushed hot, and his balls tingled. Realizing he was damn close to blowing his load for the second time in twenty minutes, he snapped his head back. His hold on Eion's hair kept the other man's lips from following.

Castrose took in the glazed, hungry expression on Eion's face as well as his wet, kiss-swollen lips. The man in his arms would never be called pretty. His features were rugged, and his body was toned and strong.

That made him that much hotter to Castrose.

In the past, when he'd gone to bars and clubs to get his rocks off, he'd always been hit on by twinks. He'd always had to be careful with his size and strength. This man, however, this shifter — *god, am I really starting to believe this shit* — would be able to handle him and all his aggression.

Eion grinned, his green eyes twinkling. "Something you want, Cass?" he asked, his voice deep and gruff, betraying his own need.

"Yeah."

Castrose had never had a nick-name before. He wasn't certain how he felt about it. Even Clayton had always called him his full name.

"Well, let's get to it then, mate." Eion gave him a cheeky leer. He squeezed his chute muscles again. "Because I'd sure love to feel somethin' other than your finger in me."

More than onboard with that, Castrose eased his digit out of Eion. His thoughts about a nick-name could wait. His dick needed his attention more. Easing his grip on Eion's hair, Castrose slid his right hand to his hip and urged him backward a step.

"Come with me," Eion urged, grabbing Castrose's hand as he began to turn.

Castrose eased off the stool and followed, allowing Eion to lead him. His gaze strayed to the leaner man's ass. The man seemed completely comfortable in his nudity as he sauntered through his home. Eyeing Eion's flexing globes and strong back muscles, Castrose decided the man certainly didn't have anything to be shy about.

"See somethin' ye like?" Eion teased, glancing over his shoulder at him.

Growling, Castrose reached out and swatted one cheek. "Yep."

Eion laughed and bounced a step forward. "Better hurry up then." With another chuckle, Eion released Castrose's hand and skipped a few steps forward, making his ass cheeks bounce deliciously. "We wouldn't want your lovely cock to feel deprived."

Then Eion disappeared into the bedroom.

At the view of Eion's flexing ass, Castrose had been riveted to the spot. His cock had throbbed, and he'd reached down to pump himself, needing stimulation in the worst way. Only when the spectacular view disappeared did he manage to come out of his daze.

Castrose snorted under his breath as he stalked forward. His grin stretched his lips, and he couldn't remember the last time he'd had fun with a lover. In fact, he couldn't remember having a lover . . . ever.

He'd had hook-ups.

To Castrose's surprise, the idea of walking away from Eion and going back to that life caused a pang in his chest.

Weird.

Then all thought fled as he entered the room, and he nearly swallowed his tongue. He had to grab the doorframe as he swayed. He'd thought he was hard before, but at the gorgeous view before him, his cock throbbed and his balls tingled, threatening to spill his seed untouched.

Eion rested on the bed on his knees. His legs were spread wide, and his ass was in the air. With his back arched, Eion reached behind himself with one hand and already had two fingers in his ass.

"Holy shit," Castrose gasped, gripping the base of his erection and squeezing . . . hard. "Fuck, Eion."

"Oh, yeah, Castrose." Eion peered over his shoulder at him

a devilish smile curving his lips. "That's what I want. You to fuck me." He wiggled his hips as he plunged a third digit into himself. "Get up here, big guy."

Castrose moaned. More than on board with that, he hurried forward and climbed up behind the other man. He rested his palms on Eion's ass cheeks and pried them apart as he watched the other man finger himself.

Watching Eion's fingers stretch his ring, Castrose panted harshly. His mouth watered with his desire to bite the man's ass. He wanted to mark and claim, drive into the man and feel his heat over and over. Castrose thought nothing would be better than his name tattooed on Eion's ass.

Shit! Where are these thoughts coming from?

Even feeling unsettled, Castrose wasn't going to miss the chance of mounting the man spreading himself for his taking. After swallowing hard, getting moisture to his too-dry throat, he rasped, "Condom?"

Eion's fingers froze halfway in his channel. Peering over his shoulder, he met Castrose's gaze. He licked his lips, then shook his head.

"I'm a shifter, remember?" Eion cleared his throat, then added, "I can't get or give human diseases. You can take me bare."

Castrose stared at Eion, reading his expression—hopeful, beseeching, and worried.

"I have a couple in the drawer, but they may be a little old." With his cheeks blazing, Eion admitted, "It's been a while." After another second of hesitation, he murmured, "We really don't need them."

With his cock throbbing and leaking with his need, Castrose struggled to decide. An old condom or bareback? His gaze lowered to Eion's hole, still stretched by the handsome man's fingers. Slick gleamed on those digits and around his hole.

If Castrose accepted a bare fuck, did that mean he accepted

the truth of Eion's words? *Could all this truly be real?* Finally, for just a few seconds, Castrose allowed himself to ruminate on the images that he'd been ignoring all day.

I saw that wolf turn into Eion. It's all real.

"Castrose?"

Eion's worried voice coupled with seeing him ease his fingers out pulled Castrose from his thoughts. Snapping his attention back to Eion's face, he saw the concern there. That wasn't what he wanted . . . to ruin the mood.

"Castrose? Are you with me?" Eion's eyebrows furrowed, and his eyes narrowed. "Is it your head? Too much activity too soon?"

Fuck. The man worries about me more than my brother . . . who I should not be thinking about when I'm about to sink my dick into another man.

"I'm okay," Castrose managed to rasp. His smile probably didn't appear too convincing, for Eion began to rock forward. Realizing he intended to flip over, Castrose grabbed his hips and squeezed. "Stay there." His voice came out gruffer than he'd intended, but he couldn't help how much he needed relief. "Just had to decide." Castrose met Eion's gaze and saw the question in his deep green eyes. "Gonna fuck you raw. Gonna fill you with my seed."

Just saying the words out loud caused a shiver to run up his spine.

Wow!

Eion stared at him for another couple of seconds. Then he turned his head and peered down, reaching for something. Lifting that same hand, he waved that something he held.

Lube.

Castrose took that as acceptance and hummed, grabbing it. After popping the top, he poured a liberal amount onto his palm. He used his thumb to close the flip-top lid as he gripped his erection with his slicked-up hand.

Growling with pleasure at the stimulus, Castrose slowly

jacked himself. He released himself after a couple of strokes and squeezed the base, easing his need for release. After getting sucked off in the kitchen less than an hour before, Castrose could hardly believe he was so on edge again.

But I am.

Lowering his gaze to Eion's ass, Castrose tossed aside the lube and settled his clean hand on the small of his lover's back. He rubbed up and down, teasing at his tailbone, enjoying the way Eion canted his hips in encouragement. When Eion groaned and glared over his shoulder at him, Castrose grinned back. At the same time, he palmed the smaller man's cheek and pulled it aside, allowing him to see his stretched star.

Damn, I want in this ass.

Castrose pushed his still-slick fingers into Eion's chute, first two, then three. When he took them easily, he carefully added a fourth. He knew he was a big man, and while he desperately wanted to fuck Eion hard, he didn't want to hurt him.

"Oh, damn, Cass," Eion mumbled, rocking into his touches. "I'm ready. Hurry the fuck up already."

Chuckling roughly under his breath, Castrose eased his fingers out. He grabbed the base of his prick and guided his crown to Eion's hole. Squeezing his cock to ease some of his rising need, he pressed against the other man's opening, holding his breath as he watched the stretched muscle give way.

Chills shot down Castrose's spine as he saw and felt Eion's body open to him. The heat and pressure felt exquisite clamping around his crown . . . then his stalk as he sank balls deep in one long, slow glide. Once his testicles were flush to Eion's body, Castrose forced himself to still.

Castrose shuddered as he levered over Eion. Resting his forehead against the smaller man's nape, he huffed out the breath he hadn't realized he'd been holding. When he inhaled again, he realized there were spots dancing across his vision.

Chuckling roughly, Castrose began breathing regularly

again. "Holy fucking god," he mumbled around clenched teeth. "You feel so damn good." With his clean hand on the comforter, holding his weight so he didn't crush the other man, Castrose wrapped his right hand around Eion's waist and slowly mapped the ridges of his man's abdominals. "Gonna stay right here a sec."

Eion moaned, trembling in his hold. "You're resting against my prostate," he said on a whine. "Gods, stay there as long as you want."

Unable to help himself, Castrose chuckled roughly. He grinned at the sweat-dampened skin less than an inch from his face. Dipping his head, he pressed a kiss to the flesh, realizing he couldn't ever remember laughing — in any capacity — during sex.

Castrose felt Eion tighten and release his inner muscles, and he groaned. All thought of past lovers disappeared as his need to rut overwhelmed him. He gritted his teeth as he fought for control while easing his erection ever-so-slowly out of Eion's exquisite sheath.

Lifting up just a little, Castrose peered between them, admiring the way his thick shaft stretched his lover's ring. As he pushed back forward, sinking his swollen length into the body beneath him, his breath caught in his chest. His lover's body opened so beautifully to him, sending delicious tingles up his scrotum and through his groin.

Giving in to his need, Castrose picked up his pace. He pressed his chest flush to Eion's back as he hammered his cock deep into his lover over and over. Heat coiled through his limbs as the dark tingle of his orgasm began to furl though his body.

Castrose growled low in his throat as the sounds of Eion's groans filled the room. He reveled in the way his lover bucked under him, meeting him thrust for thrust. Their slicked skin slid against each other as the sounds of flesh slapping together filled the room with the most erotic of songs.

Feeling the tell-tale tingle at the base of his spine, Castrose realized he was quickly coming to a head. He slid his still slightly slicked fingers around Eion's shaft. Needing his lover to join him in ecstasy, he jacked him swiftly in time with his thrusts.

"Cass!"

Eion groaned and growled in his hold, his body twitching and shuddering. His erection thickened and pulsed in Castrose's grip. Castrose swiped his palm over Eion's spilling dick, catching a load of jizz, then returned to jacking him, spreading the cum over his lover's shaft.

The feel of Eion's inner muscles fluttering with each of his spurts yanked Castrose over the edge. He opened his mouth on a shout, crying his lover's name as he rutted once, twice. Then he buried his erection deep into his lover's willing body.

As trembles racked Castrose, his cum bursting from him, he felt the warmth of his seed filling Eion. The fact that he was breeding his lover flitted through his blissed-out mind. His senses floating on endorphins, the need to externally mark his lover flooded him.

Castrose wrapped his jaw around where Eion's neck met his shoulder. Biting hard, he knew he drew blood when the tang of iron oozed across his tongue. When Eion barked a cry and jolted beneath him, Castrose realized what he was doing and jerked his teeth from his lover's flesh.

To his surprise, Castrose felt a wealth of smug satisfaction upon seeing his teeth marks in Eion's neck. He dipped his head and lapped at the blood filling the grooves. Humming at the taste of Eion's blood, he wondered why he wanted more instead of finding it disgusting.

Then Eion groaned beneath him and shuddered . . . hard.

That caught Castrose's attention. "Are you okay?" After

suckling lightly on the bite wound he'd created, catching more oddly tasty blood, he asked, "Did I hurt you?"

Stupid question. Of course I hurt him. I bit him!

Except, wait.

Eion's dick, which he still held in his right hand, was pulsing and twitching once more.

"Oh, fuck. Did you just come from my bite?"

Eion chuckled roughly as he nodded. Turning his head, he gave Castrose a loopy-looking smile. "Hell yeah. That was amazing." Sighing, his words slightly slurred, he added, "Heard the biting between mates was phenomenal. Out of this world amazing."

"Really?"

His eyes narrowing, Eion hummed. "Mmm-hmmm." A feral smile curved his lips as he eyed Castrose's neck. "Wanna feel it?"

Castrose hesitated.

Biting was part of bonding, right? Did he want that? Had he already started their bonding because he had given in to his weird base instinct?

While Castrose struggled with his decision, Eion reached back and teased along the side of his neck. His light touch caused the hairs on his neck to stand on end, and goose bumps rose on his arms. Even his nipples beaded as a feeling of anticipation thrummed through him.

It was then he realized, between his brother being here and this man under him, Castrose wasn't leaving the area any time soon.

Castrose would have plenty of time to figure things out between him and Eion. His dick twitched where it was still encased in his lover's body.

God, that feels good.

"Okay."

CHAPTER EIGHT

Eion could hardly believe his ears. "Okay?" he asked, needing to confirm.

Castrose nodded. "You bite me, I orgasm. Right?"

"It also starts our bond between us," Eion had to point out, his mind clearing. He'd made the offer on an orgasm-addled whim. Eion certainly hadn't thought Castrose would accept, so he needed his mate to understand the implications. "If we do that, I'll . . ." Eion hesitated, remembering how Castrose had responded when he'd said he couldn't ever allow him to leave him.

"You'll never let me go," Castrose finished for him.

Eion winced even as he nodded.

Castrose snorted as he leered down at Eion. "Don't think I don't get that you already feel that way."

Feeling his cheeks heat for a reason other than arousal, Eion lifted one shoulder in a half-shrug. What could he say? It was the truth, after all.

Narrowing his eyes, Castrose leaned closer, stretching his big body over him so his cheek pressed against Eion's. "I get it, and we'll talk about all the implications later when I'm not thinking with my dick." Castrose nipped at Eion's earlobe. "Right now." His mate's breath was hot against his flesh. "Bite me. I wanna fill your ass with more of my seed."

Eion groaned, knowing he could do little but obey his mate's request. Twisting his torso awkwardly beneath Castrose, he arched his neck. The position wasn't ideal—in fact, it was damn uncomfortable, especially since he had to make certain his human's long, hard erection didn't slide from his chute—but Eion opened his mouth and found purchase on the skin of Castrose's shoulder.

After a second of hesitation, Eion sank his teeth deep into Castrose's flesh. He moaned upon tasting his mate's bittersweet, life-giving fluid. Licking around where he'd embedded his teeth, he hummed appreciatively at the flavor.

To Eion's pleasure, Castrose shuddered and groaned as he clutched him even tighter. His arms were around Eion's torso as his hips bucked once, twice, then stilled. He felt Castrose flood his channel with another load of jizz.

Before he could lose his balance in the awkward position—especially since Castrose wasn't a light man by any stretch—Eion eased his teeth from his mate's neck. He lapped at the wound a couple of times, sealing it. Then he straightened under Castrose and moaned as he flopped onto the mattress, his mate following him down.

Castrose sprawled over Eion's back. His prick remained deep inside his body, and he eased his arms out from around him. As Castrose nuzzled his neck and behind his ear, humming contentedly, he slid his hands up Eion's arms until their fingers met.

Sliding his digits into Eion's, Castrose rumbled gruffly, "Damn, Eion. You weren't kidding." He nipped at Eion's earlobe, then suckled on it, easing the sting. "That was amazing."

A rough chuckle escaped Castrose as he squeezed their twined fingers. Then he licked at Eion's flesh, causing goose bumps to pimple his skin. Then he relaxed, for all the world behaving as if he were settling in for a rest while sprawled on top of Eion and with his dick still in his ass.

Eion couldn't say he minded. There was something about being covered in his mate's scent, in feeling his big body blanketing him, that settled his restless wolf. While his animal still wanted to finish claiming their human, having a happy-smelling, relaxed mate in their bed calmed his need.

They lay in silence for several long minutes, and Eion enjoyed the easy comfort between them. Every few seconds, Castrose would rub his cheek over Eion's shoulder or snuffle at his neck. If he were a cat shifter, Eion would have been certain his mate was marking and scenting him.

As it was, Eion loved it regardless.

"Am I crushing you?" Castrose's deep voice finally broke the silence followed by the man kissing his nape. "I can move."

Squeezing Castrose's fingers, Eion turned his head, lifted it a smidge, and pressed a kiss to the underside of his mate's jaw. "I'm good." When his mate lifted and turned his head, meeting his gaze, Eion grinned as he waggled his brows. "I told you, you're welcome to stay buried in my ass for however long you'd like." Squeezing his chute muscles, Eion added, "I like how you feel inside me."

Castrose sighed deeply. "So, maybe now would be a good time to tell you I'm an assassin. I specialize in long-distance kills, a sniper." He licked a stripe up Eion's neck, distracting him from responding. Then Castrose continued, "Probably should have told you that before I let you bite me. My brother decides which contracts I take. Makes sure the target needs to be offed." His big shoulders slid across Eion's own, telling him that Castrose shrugged. "Otherwise I'd take whatever contract offered the most money."

Eion swallowed hard, processing what Castrose had just admitted. His mate was a cold-blooded killer. While Eion hadn't understood the extent of Castrose's break from morality, he had at least heard his profession from his alpha.

His voice gruff, Castrose asked, "Are you gonna have a problem with that?"

Realizing he'd remained silent too long, Eion turned his

head and again pressed a kiss to Castrose's jaw. "Not a problem in the sense you mean," he began slowly, mentally working through how to explain. "You see, Alpha Declan already explained the dynamic between you and your brother."

"He did?" Castrose slid his cheek to Eion's shoulder and met his gaze. His brows were furrowed in confusion, which was also evident in his scent. "When? How would he even know?"

"Your brother has been living with Beta Dixon for almost a week," Eion explained, smirking. "Clayton thinks shifters are damn fascinating. He's already met almost everyone in the pack just to see if he's mated to one." Shaking his head, Eion felt a measure of sadness. "Unfortunately, no dice." Another thought struck him. "Damn, is he going to be jealous of you."

Castrose grunted as he finally, slowly, levered off of Eion.

Eion hissed as he felt his mate's soft dick slip from his ass. A second later, he registered the warm gush of seed oozing from his channel. As Castrose flopped sideways, lying on his side to face him, Eion noticed something else — something that hadn't penetrated his contented lethargy.

I'm in the wet spot.

"That's an odd notion," Castrose commented as he propped his head on his hand.

"What's an odd notion?" While Eion had no desire to clean Castrose's delicious scent from his body, he needed to wash up. A quick glance at his mate's groin, which was covered in residual traces of semen and lube, told Eion that his human was in the same boat. "Come on," he urged, sliding to the side and off the bed. "Let's get cleaned up."

Castrose eased off the bed, then swept his gaze over the comforter. "We made a mess."

Eion spotted the half a dozen damp spots and chuckled. "But it was so worth it," he declared as he clenched his chute muscles, enjoying the residual burn from having been stretched so damn well by his mate. Seeing Castrose's look of concern as he continued to eye the comforter, Eion told him, "I have a quilt we can use while that's washing."

Then Eion grabbed Castrose's hand and led him out of the bedroom and into the bathroom. He reached into the shower stall and turned on the water. After adjusting it to his normal temperature, he climbed inside, tugging Castrose in beside him.

Noticing the tension in Castrose's shoulders and the stiffness of his stance, Eion cocked his head. "You okay?" he asked as he grabbed the loofah and body wash.

"Never showered with anyone before," Castrose mumbled, crossing his arms over his chest, his discomfort clear.

Eion poured the body wash onto the loofah, then placed the bottle back onto the shelf. "This is just for washing up, Cass," he told him, reaching out and resting the loofah on his shoulder. "Just relax." Grinning as he swept his gaze over Castrose's body, allowing his desire to burn in his eyes, Eion refocused on his mate's face. "We'll take a playtime shower another time."

Sliding the loofah down Castrose's tense arm, Eion used his other hand to urge his human to uncross his arms. "There ye go," he crooned once his man's arms hung loose at his sides. "We won't be long in here today. We need a little more sleep tonight after all." Eion couldn't help the way he scowled as his thoughts turned to tomorrow's activities.

"Something just popped into your head that irritated you," Castrose commented, lifting a hand and rubbing his forefingers along the bridge of his nose. "What's wrong?"

Eion snapped his focus to Castrose's narrow-eyed expression. "Hmm, just thinking about my brother borrowing my motorcycle," he admitted, impressed that his mate had picked up on his sudden mood swing.

"Don't like loaning your bike?"

Shaking his head, Eion admitted, "Brennan is not a good

driver."

"Then why do it?"

As Eion cleaned, keeping his movements utilitarian, he explained about the bet and his brother's request. He dropped to one knee and worked down Castrose's left leg, cleaned his feet, between his toes, then worked up his right leg. All the while, Castrose rested his hands on his shoulders for balance.

After a perfunctory sweep over Castrose's cock and balls, earning a grunt from his mate, Eion moved up his torso to wash the rest of him. His mate lifted his arms and rested his palms on the shower walls, giving him access to his arms and pits. Eion smiled, pleased that Castrose had overcome his reticence so swiftly.

"So don't give him your bike," Castrose commented absently as he took the loofah from Eion. He grabbed the body wash and poured some on there. "Or tell him it was stolen or something."

Eion shivered as Castrose began rubbing the loofah over him. Enjoying his lover's ministrations so much, it took him a second to process his words.

It seems Castrose's lack of ethics extends to every area of his life.

"Well," Eion began slowly, trying to choose words that wouldn't offend Castrose. While Alpha Declan had given him background information on the human, Eion still technically didn't know the man. "For one, I don't squelch on bets. Second, he's family, and we don't lie to each other." After seeing Castrose's eyes narrow, Eion quickly added, "Also, as a wolf shifter, Brennan would be able to scent a lie. Paranormals can do that, you know."

Castrose remained quiet for a moment as he cleaned Eion's cock and balls.

Eion curled his toes at the pleasant stimulus, fighting his body's desire to once again harden. As a shifter, he would have a heightened sex drive until they finished bonding. Even after that, a touch from his mate would rev him up in the blink of an eye.

"Why does he want your motorcycle?" Castrose asked as he began rubbing over Eion's chest, scraping over his nipples, causing them to bead. "And why doesn't he go buy his own?"

Gritting his teeth, Eion swallowed so hard his Adam's apple bobbed. He managed to get enough moisture into his throat to rasp, "He doesn't really want one. He just wants to impress a girl." Taking a step backward, he muttered, "I'm clean."

Castrose nodded as a snicker escaped him. "We do weird shit for family. Ready for bed?"

Eion was more interested in tapping Castrose's ass, but he nodded anyway. "Definitely."

As Eion turned off the water, he saw Castrose open the door and reach for a towel. To his surprise, his human turned and wrapped it around him. Then he grabbed a second towel for himself.

Huh. He's got a caring gene after all. I wonder if that only extends to his brother and his mate.

Time would tell how his human would fit into the pack.

After drying off, Eion hung up his towel and padded naked out of the bathroom. He ignored the way his skin goose bumped. Yanking the comforter off, he balled it up.

We'll have to remember to stock towels in the bedroom.

When Eion turned, he realized Castrose hadn't followed him. He frowned, worry filling him. Carrying the soiled comforter out of the room and down the hall, Eion found Castrose picking up the quilt off the sofa that he'd been using earlier.

Damn. Is he about to refuse to sleep with me?

Then Castrose tossed the comforter over his shoulder and headed toward the hall. He paused next to Eion and skimmed his fingertips up his hipbone. With a grin, he flipped the tip of Eion's flaccid penis before sauntering past him.

Eion groaned as he rolled his eyes. Then he continued to the laundry room. After starting the washer and measuring the detergent, Eion shoved the comforter into the machine.

Hustling back to the bedroom, Eion paused in the doorway and smiled. He stared for a few seconds, appreciating the sight before him. His mate lay sprawled on his bed, the quilt halfway up his waist, leaving his gorgeous torso on display. He had one arm flung over his head and the other resting on his stomach. His eyes were closed, and his breathing was slow and even.

Gods, he's a beautiful man . . . and all mine. Or he will be soon.

"Stop staring and come to bed," Castrose ordered, cracking open his left eyelid. He used the hand on his stomach to flip up the left side of the blanket and sheet.

More than happy to do just that, Eion rounded the bed and crawled under the covers. He eased close to Castrose, but he paused before touching him, uncertain of his receptiveness. To Eion's pleasure, his mate slid his arm under his shoulders, then used the hold to pull him close, rolling toward Eion as he did so.

Eion found himself the little spoon. As the shifter in the pairing, he hadn't expected for that to happen. Still, if the position made his mate happy, Eion was fine with it.

"Never slept with anyone before," Castrose mumbled, his warm breath ghosting across Eion's skin.

Unable to help himself, Eion muttered back, "And you'll never sleep with anyone else again."

Castrose grunted.

Eion waited for more, but it wasn't forthcoming. Instead, a moment later, Castrose's breathing evened out, indicating that he slept.

Smiling to himself, Eion closed his eyes as one thought flitted through his tired mind.

That wasn't a no.

CHAPTER NINE

Castrose woke to the smells of coffee, bacon, and something else. Rolling over, he reached for Eion, but the sheets were cool. Growling under his breath, he glared at the empty side of the bed where Eion had been when he'd drifted off to sleep.

Even though Castrose had never slept with anyone before, he'd felt a supreme sense of satisfaction at cuddling the smaller man. He smiled as he sat up, recalling Eion's possessive words. While he'd mentally agreed, he hadn't voiced the thought out loud.

As far as Castrose was concerned, there'd been no point. He'd already allowed the wolf shifter to bite his neck. That started the bonding, so that meant they were together.

A partner. Huh.

Castrose slung his legs over the side of the bed. Scratching his balls, he headed toward the smells. He sure hoped Eion was the source of them.

"Which cupboard are they in again?"

Upon hearing a voice he didn't recognize, Castrose paused. He turned to the dresser and pulled out a pair of sweatpants. After tugging them on, he headed out of the bedroom and crept down the hall.

Pausing at the end of the hall, Castrose pressed his back against the wall. He peered around the corner and spotted a dark-haired stranger setting plates on the table. His back was to Castrose, and he flexed his fingers. The distance was a good thirty feet, and he would have to round the counter. Could he —

"Cass, come out and meet my brother."

Castrose heard Eion's order, and his brain stalled. Just hearing his lover's accented voice caused blood to surge south, and his prick plumped. Then he processed his words.

Pushing away from the wall, Castrose strode into the room. "How'd you know I was there?" He spotted Eion at the stove on the other side of the bar so took a place on a stool. As he sat down, Castrose recalled what had happened on those same stools the evening before. His lips quirked up as he reached down and adjusted his hardening dick.

Eion grinned at him over his shoulder. "Shifters have a great sense of smell and better than average hearing." He winked before leveling a heated look at Castrose's bare chest. "Besides, I'll always be able to smell my mate when he enters the room."

Castrose nodded once, taking Eion at his word.

"Can I get you a cup of coffee?" Eion asked as he set down the spatula and turned toward him.

"No, thanks." Upon seeing the way Eion's eyebrows shot up, Castrose quickly explained, "I don't drink it."

"Damn, you're one of those?" The stranger stared at him as if Castrose had grown a second head. "What do you drink then? *Red Bull?*"

Castrose fixed his gaze on the dark-haired man. Considering the green eyes and features, he guessed the man was related to Eion in some way. With that in mind, he did his best to keep his tone civil when he answered.

"No. Hot chocolate."

The man gaped for an instant, then snapped his mouth shut only to open it again, as if he were preparing to reply.

"Brennan, stop giving my mate shit, or I'm gonna box your ears," Eion stated, turning from the stove and crossing to the counter. "I gave you the keys. Be on your way." Eion pointed toward the door. "And you bring it back without a scratch and with a full tank of gas. Get me?"

Rolling his eyes, Brennan headed toward the door. "You're such an ass before you've had two cups of coffee."

"You knew that when you came over this early," Eion grumbled, crossing his arms over his chest as he scowled at his brother. "You just wanted a chance to ogle my mate."

Brennan lifted one shoulder in a half-shrug. "Sure." He paused next to Castrose, holding out his hand. "Hi. I'm Brennan." His gaze raked over Castrose's torso in a not-so-subtle perusal. "Welcome to the family."

Castrose narrowed his eyes even as he took the other man's hand. "It's rude to check out your brother's partner," he stated bluntly, giving the man's hand a perfunctory shake before releasing him as swiftly as was socially acceptable. "I'm an anti-social asshole, and even I know that."

Tipping his head to the side, Brennan laughed, obviously unrepentant. As he started toward the door, he winked at Castrose. "Thanks, bro!" he called, opening the door.

As Brennan closed the door behind him, Eion hollered, "No drinking and driving, and not a goddamned scratch!" Then the door closed, and Eion heaved a sigh as he shook his head. "Sorry about that." He focused a wry smile Castrose's way. "He really did come here early just to ogle you. I was hoping to get him out the door before you woke up."

"It's fine." Castrose glanced toward the front of the house where he heard the roar of a motorcycle begin to fade into the distance. "Think he'll bring it back in one piece."

"No idea," Eion admitted, sounding sad. Then he cleared his throat and smiled at him. "So. Hot chocolate? I know I have cocoa powder. What do you like as the base? Milk, half and half, heavy cream?"

Castrose rested his forearms on the counter. "Half and half, if you have it."

"Sure do." Eion matched his stance, resting his hands on the counter and leaning toward him. His expression turned hungry. "Good morning, handsome mate."

Realizing what Eion intended, Castrose turned his head. "Morning," he mumbled. Upon seeing his lover stiffen, his shoulders tensing as he straightened, Castrose realized he'd given the other man the wrong idea. "I heard voices, so came out without brushing my teeth first. Give me a minute, huh?"

Eion's eyebrows shot up as a wide grin stretched his features. "You didn't seem to have a problem with that last night."

Castrose heard the teasing in Eion's tone, but it was the man's words that truly caught his attention. "Huh. You're right." While looking at it in hindsight, Castrose thought it was a little squicky. Still, Eion didn't seem to mind. "Come here."

Reaching across the counter, Castrose gripped Eion's nape. His lover came willingly, leaning toward him. He pressed his lips to Eion's, teasing and licking, enjoying the light tongue play.

Castrose hummed, happiness filling him as he pulled away. "Now it's a good morning," he stated, unable to stop his grin.

"Yes, it is," Eion murmured, smiling back at him. While tracing his fingertips down Castrose's jawline, he offered, "Why don't you go clean up. I'll get your hot chocolate ready."

"Thank you," Castrose replied. Then he cocked his head. "I can make it myself, though. I always have in the past."

"Naw," Eion said with a shake of his head. He waggled his eyebrows, probably to soften his refusal. "You can make it for both of us next time." Taking a step backward, Eion told him, "I already have breakfast almost finished."

Castrose nodded as he turned back toward the hall that led

to the bathroom. "I'm surprised Brennan didn't try to stay for breakfast." He recalled that the man had been setting the table, after all.

"He tried, but I kiboshed that idea," Eion called back. "He was setting the table to stall, so he could meet you."

Pausing at the hallway's opening, Castrose turned back to face him. "Why would he want to meet me so badly?"

Eion peered over his shoulder, giving him a wide grin. "Finding a mate is a big deal for a shifter, and he's family, so—" He shrugged again.

Castrose nodded. "Okay." Then he headed to the bathroom.

After cleaning up, Castrose returned to the kitchen. Eion pointed at the dining room table. Castrose spotted a steaming mug of hot chocolate along with a plate full of food. There were several strips of bacon, a couple of sausage links, a pile of hash browns, and three eggs cooked over-easy. On a smaller plate were several pieces of buttered toast.

"I didn't know how you liked your eggs, so I hope that's okay," Eion stated, sitting down across from him. There was a plate heaped with even more than what Eion had given Castrose placed in front of himself. "And there's plenty more. Help yourself."

Castrose nodded. "Thank you, and I eat eggs any way I can get them." After receiving a smile from Eion, he dug into his breakfast.

For the next ten minutes, Castrose filled his belly with the delicious food Eion had prepared for him. The hot chocolate tasted rich and smooth. The hash browns had just the right amount of crispiness. The sausage links were flavorful and succulent. Even the bacon had just the right amount of chewiness. Castrose slathered strawberry jam on the toast and dipped it into the yolk, enjoying the combination of flavors.

To his surprise, Castrose managed to eat everything on his

plate. He hummed as he leaned back in his chair, patting his full belly. Gripping his cocoa mug in his other hand, he lifted it to his lips and swigged back the last of it.

"There's more," Eion reminded before crunching on a piece of bacon.

Castrose chuckled, "I couldn't eat another bite."

"More hot chocolate, then?" Eion leaned back in his chair and grabbed a carafe from the counter behind him. He held it up.

Even as he groaned and licked his lips, Castrose held out his mug. "Sure."

Eion laughed. "Guess it's to your liking," he commented as he refilled Castrose's cup.

"You make a damn fine cup of hot chocolate," Castrose admitted. He couldn't remember a time when he had enjoyed the drink that he hadn't made on his own. Everyone else always made it too weak, but Eion's was damn near perfect.

After refilling his own cup, Eion set down the carafe. "So, I—" The sound of a car approaching caused him to snap his mouth shut. He rose from the table, mug in hand, and headed toward the front windows. "Now what?" After looking out, Eion started toward the front door. "I was going to ask if you wanted me to call Beta Dixon about seeing your brother, but it seems Alpha Declan is bringing him here."

"Clayton is here?"

"Probably," Eion told him. "The windows are tinted, but that's the alpha's SUV." Opening the door, he asked over his shoulder, "Didn't he say something about you seeing him today?"

Castrose rose to his feet, taking his hot chocolate with him. "To be honest, I can't remember a whole lot of the conversation I had with your alpha." He rubbed at his head, pleased that it no longer bothered him. "Between the concussion and the shock, I was a little out of it."

Eion nodded. "Makes sense." He opened the door and led the way outside. "The porch boards are cold. Do you want socks?"

Noticing Eion was also barefoot, Castrose shook his head. "I'll be fine," he assured as he stepped onto the porch beside him. Immediately, the chill of the spring mountain morning wrapped around him, causing goose bumps to lift on his skin. Eion wasn't kidding about the planks, and the cold instantly sank into his soles. "Damn," he mumbled, clutching his hot mug close.

Castrose recognized Alpha Declan but not the small blond that slid from the front passenger seat. A second later, seeing who exited the back, he dismissed the man. His slender frame appeared barreling out of the back seat, and he jogged toward Castrose, a wide grin splitting his normally serious features.

"Hey, Castrose! You're here! What took you so long?" Clayton bounced up the steps and wrapped his arms around Castrose. "Isn't this amazing?"

Castrose returned Clayton's embrace, hugging the man. "What do you mean, what took me so long?" he asked as he released his excited brother. Clayton took a step away from him, and Castrose kept his free hand on his shoulder. "How the hell was I supposed to know where you went? I had to track you through Killian."

Clayton scowled. "I left you a message on the Sanderson News message columns just like we've done before."

Groaning, Castrose stared skyward. He mentally counted to three before refocusing on Clayton. Seeing his brother's confused expression, he stalled a little longer by taking a deep swig of his cocoa.

"Clayton, I told you not to use that one anymore," Castrose told him slowly.

"What?" Clayton's brows furrowed. "When? Why?"

"Because that message board has been compromised by —

" Castrose paused, narrowing his eyes as a thought hit. "Clayton, how many times have you used the Sanderson newspaper in the last month?"

"Um" — Clayton's brows squinched as he gave Castrose's question some thought — "Twice. Once a few days before these guys showed up, and then once last week when I first arrived here."

"Shit," Castrose grumbled, restlessly popping his neck.

"What's wrong?" Eion asked, resting his hand on Castrose's upper arm and rubbing lightly.

Clayton glanced between them, his dark eyes growing big as saucers behind his glasses. "Uh, Castrose?" he mumbled, waving between them. "What's going on?"

Castrose took in Clayton's confused expression. He glanced at Eion, who lifted his brow and dropped his hand. Realizing that his lover would allow him to play it any way he wanted, Castrose smiled at the man.

"I appreciate the thought, Eion," Castrose murmured, releasing Clayton so he could wrap his arm around his shifter's waist. *Huh. My shifter. I sorta like that.* Then Castrose turned his attention to Alpha Declan. "You didn't tell Clayton?"

"Not my place to share somethin' like that, Castrose," Alpha Declan replied.

With the way the huge black man had his arm around the small blond man, Castrose guessed him to be his doctor partner, Lark. Another man stood nearby, flanking the alpha. He was also big and broad, similar to the alpha, but there the similarity ended. The guy was as fair as the alpha was dark, with pale blue eyes that were constantly moving, showing he was surveying the area.

"Castrose?"

Returning his focus to Clayton, Castrose told him, "I didn't look in that paper, because there's a terrorist group that figured out we use it."

"Hey, maybe we could share everything inside." The small blond burrowing against Alpha Declan's side offered Eion a sweet smile. "You got any more coffee, E?" He switched his attention to Castrose. "And how's your head feeling, Castrose?"

"Were you injured?" Clayton leaned closer and must have spotted the stiches at the side of Castrose's head. He gasped and grabbed his upper arm, nearly spilling his cocoa. "What happened?" Clayton then scowled at Eion. "Did he do that to you?"

"No, Clay," Castrose immediately denied. "Calm down." A cool morning breeze took that opportunity to send a chill up his spine. "Yeah. Inside." Squeezing Eion's hip, Castrose quickly added, "That okay?"

Eion nodded. "Absolutely."

Castrose allowed Eion to pull away from him, and everyone trooped into the cabin. While Eion began getting everyone coffee or another beverage of choice, Castrose sat at the table. After the big blond introduced himself as Beta Dixon, Castrose explained how he'd followed Clayton.

CHAPTER TEN

Eion listened with half an ear as he set out mugs and poured everyone coffee. After placing the cups on the table, he added the carton of half and half as well as a dish of sugar. He set the cocoa carafe near Castrose, earning him a smile from his lover.

It also caused Clayton to level a narrow-eyed gaze his way. *Huh. What'd I do to him?*

"Stop scowling at my lover, Clayton," Castrose stated, tapping his forefingers on the back of his brother's hand. "It wasn't his fault I ended up injured. I told you that."

That caused Clayton to frown at Castrose. "If he and his sister hadn't jumped out while in wolf form, then you wouldn't have been injured," he pointed out coldly. "So technically, it is his fault. I mean, geez, he shifted right in front of you without any explanation." Then Clayton glanced between them when Eion sat down next to Castrose. "And what do you mean, your lover? Since when have you ever taken on a serious relationship? It's always been just the two of us."

Ah, so that's it. I'm threatening his relationship with his brother. Shit.

Castrose chucked Clayton on his jaw as he told him, "Yes. He's my lover. I'm his mate." He glanced Alpha Declan's way. "Did you explain mates to him?"

"That I did," Alpha Declan replied. Relaxing in his chair, he had one arm slung behind Lark's seat. He held his coffee cup with his other. "And ye seemed pretty keen on meetin' all the single members of me pack, Clayton, so why the scowl now?"

Clayton cleared his expression as he peered Alpha Declan's way. "Sorry, Alpha. I—" He paused and shook his head.

"I'm not stealing your brother, Clayton." Eion decided to just get it out there and clear the air. He smirked at the small human. "In fact, you're gaining a really big family who will give you shit as much as they harass and help you."

Clayton frowned. "Why would *I* be gaining a family? Castrose is your mate. Not me."

Eion chuckled as shook his head. "But you're Castrose's brother. That means you're family, too."

"Your brother is mating into the pack," Alpha Declan cut in. "Since ye're his brother, it makes ye an honorary member, too." Then he leveled a narrow-eyed gaze the small human's way. "That also means ye have to obey the rules of the pack." Declan focused on Castrose next. "You, too."

Castrose cocked his head. "What does that mean?"

Beta Dixon smirked as he glanced between the brothers. "It means you obey orders from Alpha Declan or myself, since I'm this pack's beta." He waved his hand absently as he added, "You'll meet the enforcers before too long—Kade, Manon, Gracen, Mishka, and Artemis."

"It'll be a while before ye meet Carson, my head enforcer, however." Declan's lips thinned, betraying his displeasure. "Since for some reason, ye took a job to give someone a bomb to kill his husband, Jared."

Castrose frowned. "If my brother and I killed one of your own, why are you being so hospitable?"

Eion not only heard the disbelief in Castrose's tone, he also scented his unease.

"They're not actually dead," Clayton answered, snorting. "Jared faked their deaths before tracking down our hideout."

"Then where are they?" Castrose glanced around before adding, "And we took the contract because it was to take out a fellow assassin." He shrugged. "It was just business."

Alpha Declan sighed deeply as Lark winced. Dixon rolled his eyes before taking a drink of his coffee.

Rubbing his hand up and down Lark's spine, Declan murmured, "Jared always figured his past would catch up with him." He smirked at Castrose. "And it was personal to him, Carson, and those of us in this pack that relied on them both." When Castrose's expression turned confused, Declan added, "Deciding who lives and who dies is a responsibility someone should never take lightly."

"So I work for you now?" Castrose hazarded, glancing from Declan to Clayton and finally to Eion. "Is that what these guys are telling me?"

Eion reached over and took Castrose's hand, squeezing lightly. "More along the lines of you're currently out of work unless a special situation comes up where the pack needs your area of expertise."

Castrose harrumphed, the noise one of annoyance. "Good thing I'm rich, but damn will being retired get boring."

"We'll find something to do," Clayton countered confidently, nudging his brother with his elbow. His blue eyes twinkled behind his glasses. "Besides, it'll be fun getting to go bowling whenever I want."

"You enjoy bowling?" Dixon asked, lifting one blond brow. After Clayton had nodded, the big man stated, "I'll go. I like bowling."

"My whole family does, too," Eion added. "My niece's birthday is coming up in a few weeks. Tessa turns six. I bet she'd love to have her party at the bowling alley." He squeezed his mate's fingers as he added, "It'll be a great way for you and your brother to meet everyone in a relaxed environment."

Castrose sighed deeply as he nodded. "I suck at bowling."

Clayton laughed as he nodded. "He really does."

"So do I," Eion admitted before leaning over and pecking a kiss to his mate's pinked cheek.

"Not that I don't love the idea of going bowling with the pack," Declan cut in. "I do need to address one more thing that came across my desk this morning."

Eion felt a fissure of unease trickle down his spine. Rarely was he part of a meeting that included the inner circle. His eldest brother was the one normally involved.

Alpha Declan focused on Castrose. "You said a group of terrorists cracked yer code. Do ye recognize any of these people?" He held out his phone.

Castrose took it and scowled at the screen. "Unfortunately, I do." Tapping the phone, he enlarged a picture of a mocha-skinned male with shaggy black hair and a cold dead expression in his black eyes. "He calls himself Hodge, and he leads a group of rebels and terrorists trying to overthrow the Armenian government."

"Well, that man was part of the group we fled from, taking your brother with us," Dixon stated, leaning forward. "He's part of the terrorists that figured out your code?"

"Yes." Castrose nodded.

Alpha Declan exchanged a glance with Dixon, then met Castrose's gaze. "He's been spotted in town," he stated. "He drew the attention of a couple local detectives because he was asking questions at a diner." Shaking his head, Declan appeared less than amused. "It seems ye are these fellows' good buddies, and ye're supposed to be meeting around here to spend the week hiking, but they lost cell service so they can't contact you."

"Let me guess. The detectives are shifters," Castrose commented, smirking. "So they immediately told you."

Grinning widely, Declan nodded. "Yep. Most of the police force and firefighters in town are affiliated with my pack." Then he smirked as he added, "Hell, about a third of the town are shifters, and another several dozen are mated to them. All in all, my pack probably makes up over half the town, and the rest who live around here enjoy the privacy created by our protection." Pointing between the brothers, Declan told them, "If ye had stopped anywhere to ask if anyone had seen yer brother, I would have known almost instantly." His eyes narrowed. "And we could have avoided the whole *you pointing a sniper rifle at my house.*"

"Not to mention your head injury," Lark piped up.

Castrose chuckled low in his throat, the sound causing pleasure to warm Eion's gut. "Of course, then I might have missed out on meeting Eion," he pointed out as he leveled a heated gaze Eion's way. "And that would have been a damn shame."

"Fate and the weird way she works," Dixon muttered, glancing between them. "So, we lure them to the Union Creek Cabins and take them out there."

Alpha Declan nodded. "I agree." He turned his attention to Castrose. "They're secluded, and there's only one cabin rented right now. We can make certain the couple is away."

Dixon nodded, pulling his phone from his pocket. "I'll call Kade." He rose from the table.

"Demitri is a waiter at the diner where several of the men were spotted," Alpha Declan commented as he followed Dixon's movements with his gaze. "I'll call him and ask him to tell them that the brothers have been in having lunch a few times."

Nodding, Dixon replied, "I'll let Kade know."

"I'm going to tell Demitri that under no circumstances should he go with them, but remind Kade of the same." Declan growled under his breath. "I can just imagine those assholes trying to sweet talk pretty little Demitri into showing them instead of just giving them directions."

"Gods, can you imagine how pissed Kiernan would be,"

Lark stated softly, shaking his head. He squeezed Declan's hand as he shook his head. "He'd seriously lose his shit if anything happened."

Declan smiled at his lover as he told him, "Kiernan may be human, but that's as it should be between mates." After pecking a kiss to Lark's lips, he rose to his feet. "Be back in a minute."

Once both men were involved in their phone calls, Eion noticed Castrose rising. Lark did, too. Eion followed, as did Clayton.

"Can I check your head, Castrose?" Lark asked, pointing.

Castrose nodded. Reaching out, he grabbed Eion's hand while asking, "Are my clothes done?"

"I brought you some that would fit," Clayton claimed. "They're in the SUV. I'll get them."

The man hurried from the cabin, disappearing before Eion could tell him that he'd pulled Castrose's clothes out of the drier after he'd woken to his brother's knocking.

"Uh, if you prefer your clothes from the hike, they're sitting on top of the dryer," Eion told him, bumping his shoulder against his lover's. "I'll grab them while Lark takes a look at your head."

Castrose nodded.

When Eion began to pull away, to his surprise, Castrose tightened his grip. He reached out with his other hand and held his bicep. Stepping close, he pressed a swift hard kiss to his lips. When he lifted his head, Castrose offered him a grim smile.

"Do you have my rifle?" Castrose asked softly. "Or does your alpha?"

Eion glanced toward his laundry room before refocusing on Castrose. "It's in the laundry room, too. Tucked away. Why?"

"I'd like to inspect it after I get dressed," Castrose told him.

"Make certain nothing was damaged when I dropped it." He shook his head. "Still can't believe I fainted. Fuck."

Lark snickered softly. "Don't feel too bad." He patted Castrose's upper arm in reassurance. "I flipped out and had to be locked in a room for a couple of days until I settled down."

"Really?" Castrose frowned as he glanced in Alpha Declan's direction where he was still murmuring into his phone. "I'm surprised the alpha allowed that, seeing as he's your mate."

"I hadn't met him, yet," Lark told him as he urged Castrose to sit back in a dining room chair. "Declan was away on pack business, and Beta Shane was in charge. I was at a barbeque and saw one of the kids shift. Freaked the fuck out," he continued to explain as he inspected Castrose's head. "Anyway, this looks good. You know, if you finish your bond with Eion, you'll start healing faster."

Even when Eion had stepped into the laundry room, he had been able to hear their conversation. Handing the clothes to Castrose, he told him, "I didn't want you to feel coerced. That's why I didn't say anything."

Castrose grunted, then pointed at his neck. "I've already accepted your bite. That was me accepting our bond." Then his pale brows shot up. "Ah. You have to fuck me. Right." Glancing around the room, Castrose stated, "After everyone leaves, we'll get that finished then."

Eion's blood fired in his veins at the very idea of fucking his mate. His mouth watered as he eyed his mark on Castrose's neck. Reaching out, Eion gently traced his fingertip around it as a shiver of anticipation thrummed through him.

Growling softly, Castrose leaned away from him. "Why does that make my dick hard?"

Lark chuckled. "Your mating mark becomes an erogenous zone." He winked as he moved toward Declan, giving them the illusion of privacy. "Enjoy."

Or not.

Then Clayton barreled back into the cabin, holding a duffel bag. "Here ya go." He skidded to a stop near the table, frowning at the clothes on Castrose's lap. "Oh. You already have some."

Eion took a step back and smiled at the man. "Those were what Castrose was wearing in the woods. He might like something else," he told the smaller human.

Castrose rose to his feet, keeping the clothes tucked to his chest. With his other hand, he reached out and took the bag from his brother. "Thanks, Clayton. I'll have to go shopping eventually, after we deal with Hodge, but this will hold me over." After shifting the bag to the arm holding his clothes, Castrose slung his arm around his brother and gave him a one-armed hug. "Where are you staying these days?"

"I've been staying at Dixon's while waiting for you to come here," Clayton told him. "I figured once you arrived, we could get a house."

"Oh, right." Castrose focused on Eion. "You told me that. Think we can add an extension to this place?"

Eion opened his mouth, then closed it again. After a glance between them, he realized that, while Castrose was his mate, he and his brother were a package deal. Nodding, Eion patted Clayton's shoulder.

"Of course." Eion glanced around, thinking of his home's layout and where it would be best to put an addition. "If we—"

"You may want to think about a separate building," Dixon cut in, announcing his return. He grinned as he settled his hand on Clayton's neck. "Maybe a two-story structure? The bottom a big-ass workshop for you, then the top your own home?" When Clayton turned and peered at Dixon, his surprise was all over his face and in his scent. The beta used his hold to rock him back and forth playfully. "I remember you telling me about how you missed tinkering at my house." Then Dixon smirked as he met Eion's gaze and stated, "Unless you don't mind having some of your handheld appliances dissected across the table."

Clayton's cheeks took on a pinkish hue as he nibbled his lip. Castrose chuckled as he set the clothes and bag on the table, then crossed his arms over his chest. Meeting Eion's gaze, he shrugged before nodding.

"A separate home it is," Eion stated with a grin. Then he recalled his mate's words. "Wait a minute. What makes you think you're going to help deal with Hodge?"

Trepidation filled Eion as Castrose peered at him with surprise. "Because I am."

"No." Eion hadn't even bonded with his mate, yet. No way did he want him anywhere near danger.

Castrose sighed as he wrapped Eion in his arms. "Eion, we brought them here. They're my problem."

"They're a pack problem," Dixon countered. His grin turned feral. "But we wouldn't say no to the assistance of a sniper."

Eion groaned, realizing he had no say in the matter. "Then I'm coming with you."

CHAPTER ELEVEN

Castrose rubbed his fingertips over the stock of his rifle absently as he peered through the scope. His nerves fired through his veins in a way he'd never before experienced. He knew it had everything to do with the man lying on the rooftop next to him.

As soon as Eion had stated he would be joining Castrose on his mission to remove the threat to him and his brother, he'd tried to talk him out of it. He hadn't wanted his lover anywhere near a fight. Unfortunately, the alpha had sided with Eion.

"You are his mate," the alpha had stated, his expression serious. "And yer bond is not complete. There's no way he will allow ye out of his sight right now."

So here I am, searching for any sign of movement in the trees and hoping nothing happens to my lover.

God, that's never happened before.

"You need to calm down, Cass," Eion whispered, rubbing his back lightly. "Everything will be fine. We're good at this."

"I didn't want you involved," Castrose reminded him as he slowly panned over the trees. "You could get hurt."

Eion snorted. "I'm a shifter, Cass. I'm a lot tougher than I look."

Glancing toward Eion for an instant, Castrose took in his amused expression. He returned his focus to his job as he muttered, "If we'd finished our bond, would you have agreed to stay out of this?"

"Not a snowball's chance in hell."

As soon as Alpha Declan had gotten off the phone, he had rounded everyone up to head to the cabins. Evidently, a pair of strangers had been at the diner when he'd called Demitri, so it was a simple thing for him to give the information to the men. That meant they had to get to the cabins as swiftly as possible.

The only ones who hadn't joined them had been Lark and Clayton. Declan had taken them home. While Clayton had complained, claiming he wanted to help, Lark had assured him that staying out of the shifters' way was the best form of help he could offer right then.

Clayton hadn't been happy, but he'd conceded.

Castrose blew out a harsh breath. "That's what I figured." He'd been mentally replaying their conversations for the last half hour and something Eion had said repeatedly had stuck in his mind. "Can't keep me safe and healthy if you're not by my side in a fight, right?"

Eion grunted. "I'd prefer you don't get into fights at all, but you're my mate, so making you happy means I'm not going to ask you to change." Then he grimaced. "Much."

Chuckling low in his throat, Castrose felt his tension ease somewhat. "Well, you have to change a little, too, so I guess that makes us even."

As Eion laughed softly, Castrose spotted movement between the tree trunks. He narrowed his eyes as he panned left and right, counting. Clenching his jaw, he growled under his breath.

Then Castrose lifted his right hand and flicked the switch on the communication bud in his ear. "I have movement. Six targets. I could take two before the others hide."

"Not necessary," Beta Dixon replied through the line. "Just cover us as we round up these yahoos."

"Then what are you going to do with them?" Castrose asked curiously.

"Oh, their lives are forfeit, sure," Dixon told him. "But we'd rather not give them time to pull their weapons."

"Okay."

Castrose fell silent, watching as darkly dressed figures slipped up behind the half dozen people. In short order, the six men had been rounded up. They were stripped of their weapons and frog-marched to the clearing where they were forced to kneel before their hands and feet were trussed.

Then Beta Dixon walked down the line, yanking off their ski masks. Alpha Declan stood nearby, scowling at the group. Once all the men were revealed, Declan growled.

"Where's Hodge?" Declan demanded.

None of the men responded.

"Right here."

The accented voice sounded from behind Castrose and to his left. Peering over his shoulder, he spotted Hodge standing in a tree, a gun in his hand. That was when Castrose noticed the red dot on Eion's chest . . . directly over his heart.

Gritting his teeth, Castrose began easing to the side, intending to cover his wolf shifter lover.

"Ah, ah, ah," Hodge said with a shake of his head. "You move another inch, and I will blow away your spotter."

Castrose froze, although he couldn't stop the tensing of his muscles. Glaring, he remained ready to jump at the slightest twitch of Hodge's hand.

"Good. Now release my men, and tell me where your brother is," Hodge demanded, a cruel smile twisting his lips. "He's gonna do a little work for us."

"No, he isn't," Alpha Declan stated calmly. "And if ye pull that trigger, ye're a dead man."

Hodge barked a laugh, the cold sound echoing through the afternoon air. "You're in no position to make demands." He snapped the fingers of his free hand, and another three figures swung from one tree to another, stopping to flank Hodge and point weapons at several of them. "Now, where is Clayton?"

Castrose growled low in his throat. "My brother will never work for you," he declared, aching to cover his lover. "And I would never give him to you so you could force him."

"I'm giving you the chance to choose, Castrose," Hodge stated on a snarl, his eyes narrowing. "But I'm losing my patience. Your spotter? Or your brother?"

"You don't have to make that choice, Cass," Eion whispered, then he lunged.

As Eion sailed off the roof, Castrose froze for several heartbeats. The sound of Hodge firing his gun yanked him back to reality. Hodge wasn't the only one shooting. His three men were, too, and Declan and his people had scattered.

Castrose rolled, taking his rifle with him. Hoping Eion was taking cover in the cabin, he brought his weapon to bear. He lifted and aimed in one smooth motion. After letting out a slow, steadying breath, he squeezed the trigger.

Hodge ducked behind the tree, and Castrose's bullet splintered the wood, sending shards flying.

To Castrose's satisfaction, he heard a shout of pain, telling him at least the wood chips had hit the asshole. Shifting his aim, he fired again. With a scream, one of Hodge's men fell from the tree.

The disturbance caused by a bullet zinging through the air near his left shoulder told Castrose he needed to get moving. Planting his hiking boots on the wood shingles of the roof, he leaped to his feet. In two steps, he reached the chimney and ducked behind it.

Castrose rested his rifle against the stone and pulled out a handgun given to him by Beta Dixon. Peeking around the chimney, he saw a number of dark forms streaking across the forest floor. He noticed they had the attention of those still in the trees, seeing as the branches shifted. He spotted the flash of the gunmen's arms, and the crack of gunfire continued to fill the air.

Narrowing his eyes, Castrose took aim. He popped off a shot at the man on the left. The spray of blood across pine needles, as well as the shout of pain, drew a grin to Castrose's lips.

Hodge and his men ceased firing and tucked themselves away from his angle once more.

Castrose continued to fire, slow and steady, as he hollered, "Eion? You okay, handsome?"

Instead of a human response, Castrose heard a barking howl. The dark forms suddenly made sense. Alpha Declan and his people must have shifted to their wolf forms.

While Castrose could only guess at their reasoning—*maybe it's a beast thing*—he needed to give them time to do whatever they were planning.

"Give it up, Hodge," Castrose bellowed as he pulled a fresh clip from his back pocket. He popped the expended one and slammed the new one into place. "You're not getting out of here without answering our questions."

"I ain't answerin' shit," Hodge yelled back while his own men began firing at the dark forms again. "And neither are my men."

Castrose spotted movement to his right and watched as one by one, Hodge's men began to topple. The bound men had no chance, and the three that were trying to untie each other were down before Castrose realized what was happening. Taking aim again, he shot at the tree Hodge was hiding in, stopping his attempt to murder the three remaining hostages who were trying to slither, roll, or hump away while still bound.

"No loyalty amongst terrorists, Hodge?" Castrose called, shaking his head.

"As if assassins have room to talk," Hodge spouted.

Before Castrose could come up with a response—hell,

there wasn't much he could say about that, since in his line of work it was common knowledge that once you were in there was only one way out—death—a massive dark brown wolf bounded out from between bushes.

Castrose watched with interest, wondering what the land-bound shifter could do to men in trees. He kept up firing though, keeping Hodge and his men pinned down. To Castrose's surprise, the big animal leaped at a young sapling.

The tree bent under his weight, then snapped back. The wolf used the momentum to launch himself into the air. His big furred frame slammed into the shooter to Hodge's left, taking the uninjured man to the ground. Several more wolves—one pale blond, one dark brown, and one black one—followed suit, launching themselves at Hodge and his injured gunman.

Hodge's henchman went down under a flurry of teeth, claws, and fur. Hodge jumped to another branch, narrowly dodging the big blond wolf. He extended his arm, taking aim, but Castrose was faster.

Castrose's bullet pegged Hodge in the upper arm. The man cried out in pain, dropping the gun. Holding his arm tight to his body, Hodge jumped to another tree, using his other arm to clutch at the branches.

Shaking his head, Castrose had to admit, at least to himself, the man was a nimble bastard. He rolled to his right hip, lifted his fleet, and pushed with his free hand. Sliding down the pitched roof, he judged the distance. Castrose reached the edge and fell, hitting the ground in a crouch.

Springing back to his feet, Castrose left the downed hench-men to the wolves guarding them. He sprinted into the forest. Castrose had no intention of allowing Hodge to escape, knowing the asshole would just continue to come after him and his brother.

Castrose ducked under tree branches, leaped over rocks,

and shoved between shrubs. Spotting a flash of movement ahead as well as the sound of more gunshots—damn, he must have had a back-up weapon—he closed in on the fleeing terrorist. Dodging around trees, Castrose screeched to a halt before he stumbled into a small clearing and gave himself away.

Getting a bead on Hodge, Castrose fired.

Hodge shouted in pain as his left leg buckled, and he went down. With his right arm already injured and tucked to his body, he reached to break his fall with his left. The move caused him to drop his gun, and the weapon bounced off a boulder and off to the left.

Shifting his right leg under him, Hodge went after it.

"Don't move," Castrose ordered, sending a bullet into the ground near Hodge's stretched hand.

Freezing—well, most of him—Hodge peered over his shoulder at him. He glanced from his face to his gun and back again. His lip curled into a sneer.

Hodge's expression cleared as quickly as it had formed. His focus darted left and right, and Castrose heard why, but he didn't bother looking. The low growls of several wolves closed in on them.

Even though the hairs on his nape stood on end, Castrose reminded himself that shifters were sentient in animal form. The wolves were the good guys. He swallowed hard, forcing himself to keep his stance relaxed.

"Come on, man," Hodge muttered, his fingers twitching. "Let me get my gun. Help me shoot these motherfucking wolves!"

Castrose chuckled low in his throat, amusement filling him. Shaking his head, he smirked.

"This ain't funny, man!"

"It is, actually," Castrose replied, lowering his firearm and slipping the safety on.

Hodge must have taken that as permission to go for his

gun, but he was far too late. A medium-sized, dark-blond wolf stood over the weapon. With teeth bared and ears pinned, the animal snarled at him.

Cursing softly in his native language, Hodge stared wide-eyed at Castrose. "How you doin' this?" He whispered the words. Then his eyes narrowed. "You trainin' wolves out here?" Hodge glanced around again, then leveled a huge grin on Castrose. "I can pay you for 'em. We're well funded. I'll leave your brother alone, too. Trained wolves could help in so many ways that a bomb couldn't."

"Stop talking," an accented voice ordered coldly.

Castrose peered to the right. Unable to help himself, he lifted one brow. Alpha Declan stalked toward Hodge, and he was naked as the day he was born, his dick swingin' in the wind.

Huh.

"What the fuck?" Hodge squeaked.

Clearing his throat, Castrose returned his focus to Hodge as he fought against the heat threatening to rise in his cheeks.

I am not gonna blush, dammit.

"You are a terrorist trespassing in my territory," Alpha Declan stated, his gray eyes narrowing as he crossed his arms over his chest. "And ye were trying to kidnap people who are part of my pack and under my protection. Do ye know what the penalty for that is in the paranormal world?"

"Para-what?" Hodge's eyes were wide in his pale face. "Pack? Territory? What the fuck are you talking about? Penalty?"

"As alpha of this pack and leader of my territory," Alpha Declan continued, not bothering to give much of an answer to Hodge's sputtered questions. "I can make yer penalty whatever I want it to be." Then his eyes narrowed. "You and yer men will be taken deep into the mountains and executed, and if yer bodies are ever located, it will be reported as an animal attack." Declan's smile turned hard as he rolled his big shoulders in a shrug. "Tragic. So many hikers try to get too close to wildlife, or campers don't properly store their food."

"You can't do that," Hodge cried, shaking his head. "I know you're a park ranger. You're required to turn me into authorities. I—"

"A park ranger is great cover, isn't it?" Declan cut in. Holding out his hand to Castrose, he asked, "May I have yer gun, please?"

Castrose handed it over.

As Declan strode closer, Hodge cringed away from him. That didn't stop the alpha from leaning close and slamming the butt of the gun onto Hodge's head. The man crumpled.

Declan straightened and smiled at Castrose. "Thank ye for yer assistance, Castrose. We appreciate it."

Nodding, Castrose worked hard to keep his focus on the alpha's face. "Happy to. It was fun." It had been, too. *Well, other than* – "Is Eion okay?"

Castrose started as he felt something press against his upper thigh. Looking down, he spotted a medium-sized, black-furred wolf. He almost backed away, but then he peered into the animal's eyes—his gorgeous, intelligent green eyes.

"Eion?"

The wolf nuzzled his thigh, its tongue lolling.

"That is Eion, aye," Declan confirmed.

Lowering his hand, Castrose caressed the fur on Eion's big head. The canine tipped his head, pushing into his scratches. When the wolf nuzzled his nose into Castrose's crotch, he took a step back with a laugh as he pushed Eion's head away.

"Knock that off," Castrose ordered with a gruff chuckle.

"Maybe ye'd best be off back to Eion's," Alpha Declan encouraged, amusement filling his tone. "You need to complete yer bond."

Castrose nodded. His blood heated and flowed south as he

thought about what that entailed. His body was more than on board with that.

Controlling himself, Castrose refocused on Alpha Declan. "What's going to happen to Hodge and his men?"

"Just what I said," Declan told him without a hint of remorse. "They'll end up a missing person statistic." Then a hardness entered his tone. "After I question them and make certain no one else will be coming after you. You're one of us now." Then Declan grinned widely and stated, "Welcome to the pack."

A warm sensation oozed through his chest—gratefulness mixed with a sense of belonging.

Huh. Family.

"Thank you." Castrose turned away, grinning at Eion's wolf form. "Come on, pretty wolf. We have somewhere to be."

Castrose couldn't stop grinning, anticipation thrumming through him, as he returned to the cabins, snagged his rifle, and watched Eion return to his human form.

Then Eion drove them home.

CHAPTER TWELVE

Eion levered over Castrose, licking and mapping the knobs of his human's spine with his tongue. His wolf's need to mount and claim his mate rode him hard, and he barely managed to keep it in check. He refused to hurt Castrose as he eased a third finger into his chute.

Lying on that roof, hearing Hodge issue the ultimatum—Eion or Clayton—made Eion come to a harsh realization. At that moment, he had been a liability to Castrose. Eion had only one recourse—remove himself from the equation.

Leaving his mate on that roof alone had been the hardest damn thing Eion had ever done. As he'd slid off the roof, landed on the ground, and leaped through an open cabin window, he had prayed to the Fates that his mate would be okay.

Thank the gods they said yes.

Castrose growled, rocking beneath his touch. "Hurry the fuck up, Eion," he demanded. Peering over his shoulders at Eion, he met his gaze with a hungry one of his own. "I'm not made of glass. Pull your fingers out, shove your dick in me, and make me yours."

His wolf howled in his mind, demanding submission.

Seeing as his wolf and his mate were on the same page—fuck and finish their bond—Eion obeyed. He eased his fingers partway out, then pushed them in again to test Castrose's body's resistance. Hearing another growl rumble from his mate, Eion slipped his fingers free.

Eion grabbed his throbbing erection and jacked himself, using the remaining lube on his fingers to slick himself up.

100

Gripping Castrose's hip with his free hand, he kissed the head of his erection against his human's stretched hole. He rubbed up and down his lover's spine as he slowly thrust forward.

As soon as Eion's crown slipped past the first ring, he heard Castrose's hiss and froze. He levered over his mate, resting his weight on his left hand. At the same time, Eion rubbed up and down Castrose's spine, hoping to soothe his mate.

"Push," Castrose ordered even as he rocked backward.

"Easy. Keep breathing for me," Eion ordered on a groan as he wrapped his right arm around Castrose's torso. Having heard the way Castrose spoke through gritted teeth, he nibbled on his mate's shoulder as he added, "I don't wanna hurt you."

Castrose lowered to his elbows, arching his back. His torso rose and fell in heaving breaths. He even swallowed so hard Eion could hear it.

Needing to ease his mate's discomfort, Eion skimmed his palm up and began plucking at Castrose's nipples. He scraped his nails over his pectorals as he worried the flesh between his teeth. His mouth watered with his urge to bite, but he resisted.

Soon.

Once Eion felt the tension in Castrose's body ease, he began to push forward again. Keeping up his ministrations to soothe his mate's virgin ass muscles, he hummed in encouragement. He licked a line of Castrose's neck and focused on the sensitive skin behind his ear.

Finally, Eion's own body trembling, he was buried balls deep in his mate. He gulped harshly, struggling for control. Never had he felt anything so exquisite as his mate's tight hold on his twitching prick.

"Gods, Cass, ye feel so good," Eion said on a moan, his accent thickening with his need. "Barely resisted mountin' ye on the drive home."

"Really?" Castrose mumbled.

"Yessss." Eion hissed his admission.

Eion had fought his need to strip Castrose only by remind-ing himself over and over that his mate had never bottomed before. As much as his nature drove him to confirm that his human was truly unharmed, he knew he needed to make Castrose's first time enjoyable. That meant the comfort of a bed and a shit-load of lube.

"Damn, this feels weird," Castrose muttered.

Castrose flexed and released his chute muscles.

The move yanked a deep moan from Eion's throat, and un-able to help himself, he jerked his hips, sliding his cock part-way out, then back in. The stimulation along his length caused his gut to clench, and his balls tingled.

Jolting, Castrose groaned. "Fuck! Do that again."

Eion couldn't have stopped himself even if he'd wanted to. His instinct to fuck and rut, to take his mate, overwhelmed him. He withdrew his erection until his crown tugged at Castrose's tight ring, then reversed.

Groaning, Eion gave in to his need. He picked up his pace. With each thrust, he adjusted his angle. On the third one, Eion found it.

"Yes!" Castrose cried, his body shuddering in Eion's grip. "There!"

Eion began pegging Castrose's prostate. Feeling his mate jerking and twitching in his arms created a riot of smug satis-faction coursing through him. He growled low in his throat as a zing went down his spine, and his balls tightened.

Needing Castrose to come with him, Eion slid his hand down and gripped his erection, pleased to find it straining and leaking. He jacked it in time with his thrusts, teasing his frenulum on each upstroke and twisting his tight grip on each downward one.

Castrose shouted his pleasure as his channel clamped

down on Eion's cock. "Eion!"

Hearing Castrose cry out his name sent Eion tumbling over the edge. He buried his erection as deeply into his mate as possible. His cock pulsed, shooting his seed into Castrose.

As soon as Eion felt Castrose begin to relax, he sank his teeth into his claiming mark. He swallowed his mate's sweet, life-giving fluid, then sucked for more. Heady pleasure coursed through him upon feeling his human shake and shudder. Eion still held Castrose's cock, and he grinned around the flesh in his mouth.

Hell yeah.

Castrose drooped beneath him, resting his head on the comforter. His body went damn near lax under him.

Eion eased his hold on Castrose's dick as he withdrew his teeth. Licking over his claiming bite, he sealed the wound once more. Pushing up from where he sprawled over Castrose's body, Eion gently rubbed over his side, then down his flank.

Ever-so-carefully, Eion eased his softening prick free of Castrose's body. He peered down and saw Castrose turn his head. His mate sported heavy-lidded eyes and a loopy smile, and he made no indication that he planned to move from his frog-like position.

Eion chuckled softly as he gripped Castrose's hips and gently eased him sideways. After situating his mate on his back, Eion grabbed his calves and helped him stretch out his legs. Then he slipped from the bed and leaned down, pecking a kiss to Castrose's lips.

"Be right back," Eion told him.

Castrose hummed in response.

Grinning, pride flooding him, Eion hustled out of the bedroom. He entered the bathroom and quickly washed himself up. Then he rinsed out the cloth, grabbed a dry one, and returned to the bedroom.

Castrose hadn't moved, drawing a soft chortle from Eion.

"What?" Castrose slurred the word as he eyed him.

"I love that my fucking wiped you out," Eion admitted as he crossed to the bed. He began wiping down Castrose, pleased that the man allowed him the privilege without complaint. "You're sexy as fuck like this."

Grinning and humming, Castrose pointed out, "Well, I was in a firefight today, so between you giving me a double orgasm and coming down off the adrenaline high, I'm definitely wiped." He lifted his arms and wiggled his fingers. "Come here. Nap with me."

"With pleasure."

As if I'd turn down a chance to cuddle with my mate.

Eion tossed the soiled cloths into his laundry hamper. Then he helped Castrose get under the comforter and sheet. Joining him, Eion settled against his human, sighing happily when Castrose wrapped his arms around him and pulled him so he half-sprawled over his chest.

After letting out a contented sigh, Eion whispered, "I do have one question."

"Shoot."

Tipping his head back a little, Eion met Castrose's gaze. "Why did you suddenly accept everything?" Upon seeing Castrose's furrowed brows and the light of confusion in his pale blue eyes, Eion elaborated. "You saw me shift but didn't believe, then you did. You told me you didn't believe in the mate shit, then you did. What happened?"

Castrose remained quiet for a moment, holding his gaze. Then he sighed before kicking the corners of his lips into a smile. "Easy. I don't dwell on things I can't control, but I'm damn good at accepting them." Threading his fingers through Eion's hair, he scraped over his skull lightly. "It took me a little time because I thought it was part of the concussion, but I worked it out."

"I'm glad you did."

Leaning over, Castrose took Eion's mouth in a light, sipping kiss. "Me, too." Then he relaxed and closed his eyes.

Eion did the same, drifting off to the rhythmic breathing of his mate.

EPILOGUE

The trill of Eion's phone drew him out of his comfortable slumber. The twilight rays filtering through the window told him they'd been out almost all afternoon. The phone stopped ringing, and he allowed his eyelids to slide back closed.

Then the phone started up again.

Groaning softly, Eion rolled over and grabbed the offending device from his nightstand. Seeing it was his brother calling, Eion answered.

"Hey, Cliff. What's up?"

"Come down to Colin City Hospital," Cliff stated without preamble.

Eion jerked to a sitting position. "What?" *Wait.* "Is Lisa in pre-mature labor?" He pushed aside the covers and slid from the bed.

The move roused Castrose, who stared at him for an instant before also rising.

"No. It's Brennan," Cliff told him. "He wrecked your bike."

Feeling his heart skip a beat in his chest, Eion whispered, "How bad is it?" For a shifter to end up in the hospital, it had to have been a nasty accident.

"I'm not certain, yet," Cliff admitted. "I got a call from Doctor Carmichael, so at least we know he's secure."

"Right." Eion pulled open a dresser drawer and grabbed a pair of jeans. "I'll be there as soon as possible."

The line disconnected without a good-bye, and when Eion placed his phone on the nightstand, he realized his hand was shaking.

"Damn it," Eion muttered, clenching his hand, trying to gain control of himself. "I knew I shouldn't have accepted that bet."

I knew better.

"What happened?" Castrose asked, already half-dressed.

Eion started moving again as he told Castrose what he knew.

"And Brennan being in a human hospital? Is that going to cause a problem?" Castrose commented as he plucked Eion's keys from his hand. "I'll drive. You're in no condition."

Nodding, Eion accepted that . . . especially since he didn't even comment when Castrose helped him into the passenger seat. Once his mate climbed behind the wheel and headed them toward Colin City, Eion told him, "Doctor Ailean Carmichael is a black jaguar shifter, so he'll adjust whatever records are needed to keep our secret."

Castrose grunted acknowledgment, then pointed at the GPS. "Enter the hospital information."

Eion did so, then Castrose reached over and gripped Eion's hand where it rested on his thigh. "Don't borrow trouble."

Taking that advice to heart, Eion took a few deep breaths. The earthy fragrance of his mate filled his senses. The scent caused his pulse to slow, and his body relaxed.

"There you go," Castrose rumbled, squeezing his hand and rubbing his forefingers on the inside of his wrist. "I can feel that your pulse just slowed."

"It's because of you," Eion admitted. "A mate's scent and touch soothes."

Castrose nodded. "Good."

When Castrose pulled into the hospital parking lot nearly forty-five minutes later, most of Eion's calm went right out the window. He spotted his parents striding toward the emergency entrance where Cliff waited.

"Want me to drop you off here?" Castrose asked, slowing

the vehicle.

"Yeah, thanks," Eion replied, barely waiting for the pick-up to sufficiently slow. Jogging to catch up with his family, he asked, "Have you heard anything?"

Nodding, Cliff wrapped an arm around their mother's free shoulder, since their father was holding her on the other side. Teline was cuddled against Duncan and offered Cliff a hope-ful smile. His eldest brother's distressed scent didn't put Eion at ease.

Cliff didn't explain until they'd stepped through the doors and they were joined by Lisa. Rainy, Eion's second eldest brother, was there, too, as well as Rainy's mate, Travis, who happened to be Lisa's brother. Niamh stood close to them, so Eion assumed the rest of their family was on the way.

"What happened, Cliff?" Duncan asked.

"Brennan was driving Eion's *Harley* drunk," Cliff stated, his soft voice gruff. "And he had a girl straddling his lap." He shook his head as he swallowed hard enough to cause his Adam's apple to bob. "A logging truck came around the cor-ner, but Brennan had drifted into his lane. In his impaired state, he couldn't correct in time."

Eion grimaced, guilt seeping through him. "I knew I shoulda said no."

"It wasn't your fault," Castrose stated as he slid his arms around Eion from behind, announcing his presence. "You gave him guidelines, and Brennan chose to ignore them."

"I'm sorry." Cliff wrapped his arms around Lisa, placing one hand protectively over her pregnant belly. "Who are you?"

Gripping Castrose's forearms where they crossed over his torso, Eion stated, "Everyone, this is Castrose, my mate."

Duncan held out his hand. "Welcome to the family. I'm Duncan MacDougal, Eion's father." He dipped his chin, indi-cating their mother. "This is Teline, his mother."

Castrose's scent gave away his surprise, but he reached out and shook Duncan's hand. "Nice to meet you." Releasing him and settling his arm back around Eion, he added, "Wish it was under different circumstances."

After quick introductions were done, Teline asked, "What happened to the girl? Is she all right?"

Eion couldn't help but smile. Trust his mother to worry about everyone.

Cliff nodded. "Brennan protected her. She walked away with only a little bit of road rash on her thigh." After taking a deep, obviously calming whiff of Lisa's scent, Cliff continued. "Brennan wasn't so lucky. Both his legs were broken as well as his left arm. He also sustained a head injury." Cliff's voice grew hoarse. "Doctor Carmichael has him in surgery to fix his left leg. That limb took the worst of it, shattering in a couple of places."

A whimper escaped Niamh, and she was immediately sandwiched between Rainy and Travis. When Teline sobbed softly, Duncan held her close and whispered words of comfort.

Over the next thirty minutes, the rest of their siblings arrived—Cullen and his mate, Matilda, plus their other brother Rory and sister Brielle with her mate, William, as well as Niamh's mate, Carter. They huddled in chairs, hardly talking. Each time a doctor or nurse came into the room, they would stare expectantly.

Finally, Alpha Declan arrived with Lark. He murmured his apologies for taking so long to get there, and Eion figured the delay had something to do with the men they'd captured that day. Lark gave Teline a hug, then hustled into the back with a promise of gathering information.

After another ten minutes, Lark reappeared dressed in scrubs. He beckoned them and guided everyone into a smaller waiting room on the third floor.

"Brennan has just come out of surgery," Lark explained, cuddling close to Declan's side. "They're moving him to an observation room. In about fifteen minutes, I can start taking you back two at a time, but they don't expect him to wake anytime soon." Lark hesitated an instant, then told everyone, "Right now he's stable, and Doctor Carmichael will be out shortly to explain the extent of his injuries."

Once again, they waited.

Eion couldn't begin to describe the comfort he received from Castrose's presence. He pressed close to his human's side, and his mate held him with his arm around his shoulders. Castrose rested his other hand on Eion's thigh.

Evidently, he took the news that Eion took comfort from his scent and touch very seriously.

Over the next hour, two at a time, they filtered through Brennan's room. When Eion took in the wires and tubes attached to his too-pale brother, his heart skipped a beat. Only Castrose's arm around his waist kept him on his feet.

"It's not your fault," Castrose reminded him.

Eion nodded. His mate was right, but that didn't make it any less painful.

Brennan's chest rose and fell in a steady rhythm, and he didn't have a breathing tube down his throat, so his torso was evidently fine. He prayed to the gods that the bandage around Brennan's head wouldn't leave lasting damage. After all, due to being a wolf shifter, Brennan's limbs would heal easily enough.

Settling in the chair beside Brennan's bed, Eion leaned forward. "Hey, Bren," he murmured. He rested his hands on the sheet, taking his brother's fingers in his own and squeezing lightly. "You got us all worried. What the fuck were you thinking?"

Eion winced at how insensitive that sounded and felt a bit of relief that Brennan slept.

Except, then his eyelids fluttered.

Squeezing Brennan's fingers again, Eion slid to the edge of his chair. "Hey, Bren. You with me?"

"Yeah." The word was spoken slowly, drawn-out, and in a soft hiss.

His heart rate spiking, Eion murmured, "Do you remember what happened?"

Once again, Brennan murmured, "Yeah."

Gods be praised. His head is okay.

"We're all worried about you, Bren," Eion told him, rubbing his thumb over the back of his hand, avoiding the IV port. "But you should know, as soon as you get well again, I'm gonna kick your ass for scaring us like this."

Brennan let out a long sigh, and Eion thought he'd fallen back to sleep. But a second later, Brennan whispered, "Sorry."

Eion rubbed over the forearm of Brennan's good arm. "Don't worry. Just get better." After a second of hesitation, he couldn't help but add, "You can tell us why you did it later."

"Met my mate." Brennan's words were soft and slightly slurred, but Eion could still make them out.

"What?" *Wait.* "The girl you were riding with is your mate?"

"No." Brennan's eyelids fluttered again, then opened. He stared at him with a slightly vacant gaze. "Can't have mate. Married. Kids." He heaved another sigh and closed his eyes, a tear slipping from beneath it. "I'm alone."

Eion gaped as he watched Brennan's breathing even out again.

"Holy shit," Eion whispered, his mind rolling around that information as he gripped Castrose's hand where it rested on his shoulder. When the doctor came and told him their time was up, Eion released his brother's hand and returned to the waiting room. "Hold up," Eion said, lifting his hand when he saw that Niamh and her mate, Carter, were next. Seeing her questioning look, Eion beckoned for them all to huddle close.

"Brennan woke up for just a second."

Exclamations filled the room, and Eion lifted his hands. Once everyone was quiet again, he lowered his voice and explained what his probably drugged up brother had told him. As Teline pressed her hand to her mouth, Eion realized Brennan's sudden recklessness was beginning to make sense.

"So, a married woman with kids," Castrose mused, rubbing his hands up and down Eion's upper arms. "I could take out the husband."

Cullen's brows shot up. "Take him out?" His confusion was evident. "Where? Why?"

Castrose chuckled darkly. "Not like out to dinner."

Peering over his shoulder, Eion spotted the way his mate glanced around quickly.

Then Castrose leaned close and murmured, "I'm a sniper, an assassin. I would *take care* of the obstacle to Brennan's mating."

There were a few gasps, a chuckle, a snort, and even a snicker. It was Duncan who answered, "Very thoughtful, but that's not the way we handle those kinds of obstacles, son."

"Why would you even offer?" Rory asked with obvious curiosity. "You don't even know him."

"True," Castrose replied with a nod. "But Brennan is Eion's brother. I'm Eion's mate." His big shoulders lifted in a shrug. "That means Brennan is family. We take care of family above all else."

Eion turned in Castrose's arms, wrapping his own around his lover's waist. "Thank you for the offer, but we'll find another way."

Gods, I hope there's another way.

Castrose smiled down at Eion, his blue eyes clear without a hint of guilt for what he'd just offered. He nodded. "The offer will always be on the table, handsome."

As Niamh and Carter headed to Brennan's room, Castrose dipped his head and pressed a kiss to Eion's lips. Eion opened easily, rubbing up and down his man's back. As Castrose sank his tongue into his mouth, Eion reveled in the taste of his mate . . . a new extension of their family.

The soft chuckles and low wolf whistles caused them to draw apart. Eion smiled as he gazed into Castrose's eyes. He realized that anyone who threatened his family would end up in his sniper's crosshairs.

Eion couldn't think of a damn thing wrong with that.

YOU MAY ALSO ENJOY THE FOLLOWING FROM EXTASY BOOKS INC:

Vying for His Affection
Charlie Richards

Excerpt

Rhyme had never scented blood so enticing. His stomach clenched, and his mouth watered. Need for the man before him caused his half-hard dick to thicken so fast Rhyme nearly swayed on his feet.

Gods! Could this human be my beloved?

"Oh, little bit," Rhyme mumbled. "Let's go for a moonlight ride."

"Really? What the hell makes you think I'd go anywhere alone with you?" the man snapped, resting his hands on his hips. "First you insult me, twice, and now you think I'm gonna give you the time of day?" He snorted as he turned away from him, then sauntered toward Murdoch. "Looks like you got a little pony ready for me, handsome." He stopped before the animal and eyed it somewhat warily. "What's its name?"

Rhyme's stomach clenched for a whole new reason. He hated being dismissed . . . but he hated the upset scent rolling off the sexy man even more. The human who could very well be his beloved had thought he'd been insulting him.

Shit!

When Murdoch glanced Rhyme's way, a question flashing in his eyes, Rhyme mouthed, Name? His friend and fellow vampire offered an almost infinitesimal nod before turning his attention to the human.

"This is Lily," Murdoch told him, rubbing the mare's nose. "And she's not really a pony. She's just small for a quarter horse." Holding out his hand, he added, "What's your name?"

"I'm tired of people making fun of my size," the man stated, ignoring the question and petting the horse's neck. "You're a pretty girl, Lily. Are you a nice girl?"

"She is a nice girl," Murdoch assured. "And we pulled her out to make you more comfortable, not to make fun of you." He offered a reassuring smile as he added, "We do the same for all our guests." Pointing at a huge behemoth of a man, Murdoch told him, "Just like our friend over there is paired up with that gelding on the end."

Rhyme watched the human's eyes widen as he took in the size of the horse Murdoch had pointed out. Charlie was a seventeen-hand gelding who was part quarter horse and part friesian. They'd ended up with the animal when one of their bigger mares slipped through a broken fence and got into the pen with Gypsum's stallion. The resulting foal ended up big. Fortunately, he'd been born with his mother's sweet disposition.

"You all put your foot in it," a young woman stated from where she'd stopped beside Rhyme. She smirked at him as she held out her hand. "I'm Lilibeth. Which horse is mine?"

"It wasn't intentional," Rhyme muttered, feeling his cheeks warm. Good thing his dark skin hid such things. After a quick glance over Lilibeth's frame, he pointed toward the gelding next to Lily. "That's Jake. He's a nice boy."

"You did not just check me out," Lilibeth said with narrowed eyes.

Rhyme barked a laugh as he shook his head. "No, ma'am," he immediately assured her. "Just verifying leg length and body type so I can put you in a comfortable saddle."

Lilibeth nodded, her stance relaxing. "Okay." Then she headed toward the horse Rhyme had indicated.

Over the next several minutes, Rhyme and Murdoch went through the process of assigning horses and getting everyone comfortable in the saddle. When Murdoch moved toward the little guy at the end to finish the process, Rhyme gripped his upper arm, staying the action. "This one's mine," he murmured upon seeing the fellow vampire's surprise.

"You sure?" his friend muttered back. "Doesn't seem to want much to do with you."

"I'll have to fix that, then, won't I?" Rhyme didn't extrapolate. There wasn't time. "Start the usual spiel."

Murdoch nodded and headed toward the front of the group, not questioning him again. As a lower-ranking enforcer for their vampire coven, his buddy wouldn't question him. Murdoch would follow Rhyme's orders.

"I'm sorry you thought I was making fun of you," Rhyme stated after stopping next to the man on Lily. He rested his hand on his knee and squeezed lightly. "It wasn't my intention."

The human peered down at him with narrowed eyes. "How else should I have taken being called the little stringbean?" There was a snarl in his tenor voice. "Get your hand off me."

Rhyme grimaced as he lifted his hands in placation. "Okay. You're right. That was thoughtless of me." Scowling at his memory of their first meeting, he grumbled, "And you called me oversized, so I don't know if you have any room to talk. I'm only six-foot-two."

"With a giant frame," the man pointed out, stabbing his finger in the air at his torso. "Wide shoulders, big pecs. I bet you even have a six-pack under there. Anyway, it doesn't matter. Just adjust my stirrups and let's get on with this bull-shit company activity."

Swallowing hard, Rhyme tried to figure out what he could say to mend the rift that his overheard comment had created. *If he's my beloved, shouldn't the pull to bond be working in his favor?* He'd seen it happen with other vampires.

Doing as the man had ordered, Rhyme swiftly adjusted the length of the stirrups to a more comfortable position for him. Once he was done, he couldn't resist gripping his calf and helping him get his foot in the stirrup. He squeezed lightly along the skinny calf, rubbing his thumb over the faint muscle.

"Damn, you're skinny." The words were out of Rhyme's mouth before he could stop them. All his focus was on touching the slender man on the horse before him and how it made his blood burn and thud through his veins. "So fucking—"

"Shut the fuck up," the human snarled, jerking his foot away from Rhyme's hand. "I said get your hands off me."

In the process, the man slammed his heel into Lily's side. The mare jerked and shifted sideways, instantly responding to the unexpected pressure. She didn't have far to go, considering Jake stood next to her.

Still, it was enough.

The man lost his balance and tumbled toward Rhyme, squeaking in alarm. On instinct, he caught the human. As luck would have it, the man knocked Rhyme's hat from his head with his flailing limbs, then slammed one palm into his face and the other to his shoulder.

Rhyme couldn't help but gasp, which caused his fang to scrape over the human's palm. The man's blood oozed from the scratch, filling his mouth. The sweet metallic taste caused Rhyme's vampiric instincts to flare to life as his entire body surged with hunger.

Mine!

"Let go of me, goddammit!"

Coming back to himself with a mental thud, Rhyme realized that he was holding his sweet beloved around his waist. He had his face tucked against the man's neck, and he was inhaling his scent. Rhyme even rubbed his right hand up and down his near leg, since the other one was still draped over the saddle.

Lily had calmed. Probably thanks to Murdoch, who stood at her head, rubbing her nose. His fellow vampire stared at him quizzically.

Unable to explain right then, Rhyme settled his beloved, the human he hoped to soon make his forever bonded love, back into the saddle. It took every damn scrap of self-control he had to release him.

As Rhyme nodded at Murdoch and joined him before the group, he prayed his aching erection wasn't noticeable, since his flannel over-shirt was untucked. As he listened to his fellow vampire start the instruction spiel they gave every time they took a group on a trail ride, one thought reverberated through his mind.

I met my beloved, and I don't even know his name.

ABOUT THE AUTHOR

Charlie started writing fantasy when she was eight, and after stumbling onto her first erotic romance at age nineteen, she realized her true calling. She now focuses on writing gay erotic romance, normally of the paranormal variety, with heroes of all kinds. With the help and support of her husband, Charlie finally fulfilled one of her life-long goals . . . move to acreage with her horses. You can often find her curled up with her laptop and a cup of tea or glass of wine, creating her next adventure. Charlie enjoys exploring the mountains of her new Oregon home on horseback, 4-wheeler, or motorcycle.

She can be reached at ch.richards2010@yahoo.com
Or visit her at www.charlie-richards.com